GLASSHEART

GLASSHEART

The Secrets of Eden Eld

BOOK 3

Kate Alice Marshall

VIKING

VIKING
An imprint of Penguin Random House LLC, New York

First published in the United States of America by Viking,
an imprint of Penguin Random House LLC, 2022

Visit us online at penguinrandomhouse.com.

Library of Congress Cataloging-in-Publication Data is available.

Printed in the United States of America

ISBN 9780593526422

10 9 8 7 6 5 4 3 2 1

BVG

Design by Kate Renner
Text set in Perrywood MT Std

For Mouse, again and always.

The Tale of the Brackenbeast

Once upon a time there lived three children, born on Halloween, who were cursed to be turned into a magical key by the dreadful People Who Look Away, led by Mr. January. This key would open the door to their wicked realm and unleash its horrors upon the world.

But these three children—Eleanor, Pip, and Otto—were bold and clever and persistent, and they escaped Mr. January on Halloween night. They could have saved themselves for good, but they knew Mr. January would only find other victims. So instead they made a bargain: he and his two sisters would each have one more chance to capture the children. If they failed, they would have to give up their scheme forever.

The first sister came for them with tricks and potions and beasts of mushrooms and mud. In her realm of bones and endless muck the children found a new ally: Jack, a man possessed by the strange power of a Prime Story. Three Stories there were, tales that could take a person over, erasing their memories and all they'd been: the warrior, the world-walker, and the hedgewitch. Once, Jack had another name. Once, he'd had another life. Now, nothing but Jack remained.

Eleanor was shocked to learn that Jack was her father, and devastated to discover that her mother, possessed by the Story of the hedgewitch, had lost all memory of her. And the Stories weren't done stealing people from her, for the Story of the warrior was through with Jack. It slipped from him to Pip, and as its power overtook her, she began, slowly, to change.

Once more, Eleanor, Pip, and Otto defeated the People Who Look Away, but at a cost. For now Pip bore the warrior's Story, and it was beginning to unwrite her to make room for itself. Eleanor and the others could only wait for Mr. January's second sister to come for them. But then they received an unexpected visitor: the world-walker, who came with a warning . . .

One

Eleanor Barton had just asked her aunt to pass the marshmallows when a fairy tale walked across the back lawn.

Eleanor froze, staring out the kitchen window at the tall, dark-haired woman as she lifted her hands, motes of light drifting around her like stars. There was a moment of perfect stillness, and then she began to weave the moonlight around her in a flowing dance.

This was, Eleanor thought, extremely inconvenient.

"Something wrong?" Eleanor's aunt, Jenny, asked with a troubled little frown, mini marshmallow bag still extended.

Jenny and her husband, Ben, were not exactly aware that for the past several days a woman out of a fairy tale had been staying in their house. Not just any woman: the girl with backward hands, heroine of a number of the stories in *Thirteen Tales of the Gray*. Her name was Wander, which was all she'd managed to tell Eleanor and her friends before she declared herself "weary" and fell asleep.

For four solid days.

"Nothing's wrong," Eleanor said quickly. Luckily, Aunt Jenny and Uncle Ben were sitting with their backs to the kitchen window, but Naomi, Eleanor's seven-month-old cousin, giggled madly, pudgy hands stretched toward the window.

At least this meant Wander was awake.

"You *can* talk to us, you know," Ben said. "I realize we're totally uncool adults, but we're pretty smart."

Jenny and Ben had been trying to turn Hot Cocoa Night into Tell Us Your Problems Night for months, but Eleanor couldn't exactly break it to them that her problems were less "homework is hard" and more "immortal bad guys are trying to capture me and my friends so they can get home to their freaky evil world."

"Everything is fine," Eleanor assured them, just as Jack, her father, strode across the lawn. He gestured frantically at Wander.

Wander dropped her hands, and the moonlight trailed to the ground with a sound like a violin bow sighing across the strings. Jenny started to turn to see what had made the noise.

In a second Jenny was going to see Wander. And while most people couldn't see magical things properly, or remember them once they had, that forgetfulness came at a price. Just this past spring, mud monsters had attacked the house and kidnapped Ben. Afterward, Jenny had migraines for over a month, and

Ben still woke up with nightmares—even though they didn't remember any of it.

Eleanor thought frantically. She needed to distract them. "How do you know if you like someone?" she blurted out.

Jenny's head whipped back around. "Do you have a crush, Ellie-Belly?" she asked.

"You haven't called me that since I was *four*," Eleanor complained, cheeks turning red-hot. "And no. Or maybe? I don't know." It had just been the first thing she could think of. She didn't have time for crushes. For feelings of any kind, really, other than dread and anticipation over what the People Who Look Away would try next to snatch up her and her friends.

"Who is he? Or she? They?" Ben asked. His eyes narrowed. "What are their future prospects, career-wise? Can they pass a background check? Can they change a tire?"

"Uncle Ben, I'm thirteen. No one my age can change a tire," Eleanor said, rolling her eyes. "And there aren't any criminal masterminds at my school."

Jack was herding the reluctant Wander away from the house. They were almost out of sight. Naomi gabbled and waved. Eleanor popped a cheesy puff into her hand, and Naomi shrieked in delight, momentarily distracted.

"Is it that kid who was helping you with that language arts project—what was his name—Andy?" Jenny asked as Naomi slammed the cheesy puff enthusiastically against the table. "He was super sweet. And cute, too, if I'm not mistaken."

Andy Park *was* sweet and cute, it was true. And he had sort of asked Eleanor to the spring dance, though she'd turned him down because she and Otto were spending the evening experimenting with a spell for locating lost objects. (They weren't sure if it had worked, since it had led them to an expired membership card for something called Blockbuster under the back seat of Ben's truck, which, while certainly lost, was not precisely *missed*.)

"What about what's-her-face who always waves when I pick you up?" Jenny asked. "Mabel, wasn't it? She's *very* pretty."

"She's not *just* pretty, she's also super smart," Eleanor put in quickly, because people always assumed Mabel's qualities ended at her expert use of lip gloss. Jenny and Ben gave each other knowing looks, and Eleanor dropped her head into her hands, groaning. This had been a terrible idea. Now they were going to think she had a crush on Mabel. Or Andy. And she didn't have a crush at all. Because she didn't have time for crushes, and she was probably completely doomed and wasn't going to live to see fourteen anyway, so what was even the point?

As Jenny and Ben debated the relative strengths of her "suitors," as Ben instantly dubbed them, Jack appeared at the kitchen door, looking out of breath.

"Hey, Jack!" Eleanor chirped. "How's it going?"

"Everything is under control for the time being," he said, his voice layered with meaning. He probably thought he was being subtle. Subtle was not Jack's strong suit. It wasn't really his fault—for the past forty years he'd been kind of a fairy tale himself. He even looked a lot like a fairy tale, though he'd traded his fantasy-world clothes and sword for T-shirts and jeans. He had wavy blond hair that fell around his shoulders and a neatly trimmed beard, and since the Story had left him, his eyes had turned from slate gray to a startling bright blue.

"I left your cocoa on the stove," Jenny said, standing. He waved her back to her seat.

"Please don't trouble yourself. Actually, I am afraid I must miss out on Hot Cocoa Night, and steal my daughter away as well. There is something we need to discuss."

Jenny and Ben gave each other a look—the kind that's really a whole conversation. They were still Eleanor's legal guardians, partly because Jack wasn't legally real at all, and partly because Eleanor had only known him for a few months. Before she and Pip had rescued him this spring, he'd spent her entire life submerged in mud in a magical coma.

Their relationship was somewhat complicated.

"All right," Jenny said at last. "We'll catch up on cocoa later. Don't stay up too late, Elle."

"I won't," Eleanor promised.

She left her cocoa on the counter before following Jack into the hall and then the Great Room, where he paused. "I apologize for interrupting your time with your family," he said. *Your family*, as if he didn't fit that definition. Eleanor knew it wasn't because he didn't want to be family. They hadn't had time yet to figure out who they were to each other.

Eleanor shrugged. "I was kind of glad to escape," she admitted. "So Wander is awake?"

"Indeed. She's outside, though I managed to convince her to avoid standing *directly* outside the window. She wishes to speak to you and the others. She declined to tell me why; she says she will wait for 'the real Jack.'"

That meant Pip. The magical Story that had possessed Jack for decades—that had made him forget his real name and his real life—was in Pip now. She hadn't lost her memories yet, but it was only a matter of time.

Once they were gone, the memories—and Pip—would be gone for good. Even months after the Story left him, Jack didn't remember anything about his life before. Eleanor pushed that thought away. Thinking about what was happening to Pip made her feel sick to her stomach.

"It's past curfew, but maybe Pip can come over tomorrow," Eleanor suggested, forcing herself to focus on the present.

Jack looked uneasy. "I wish I knew exactly what it is that Wander wants," he said.

"You don't trust her?" Eleanor asked, surprised. In all the tales she'd heard, they'd been fast friends.

He sighed. "Wander has always been a kind and loyal ally, but the world-walker is . . ." He waved a hand. "She sees things no one else can, and sometimes that leaves her disconnected from what is right in front of her. And she has very little sense of danger or common sense."

"Didn't you intentionally get eaten by a dragon once so you could fight it from the inside out?" Eleanor asked, raising an eyebrow.

"It was a dread wyrm. But I see your point," Jack said.

They made their way to the front door so they could slip outside unnoticed, and Jack led her around the house toward the overgrown orchard out back. The apple trees were gnarled. They seemed to clutch at the young, pale fruits jealously.

Wander knelt among the tree roots at the edge of the orchard. Her eyes were closed, and gleaming shards floated around her like a cloud of tiny stars. She had pooled the moonlight beside her on the grass and was twisting one end of it with her long, elegant fingers, spinning it into silver thread. She hummed to herself as she worked, and the sound made goose bumps prickle along Eleanor's arms.

"Wander?" Eleanor said. The woman looked up but didn't pause in her work. She had to turn her arms out to wrap the thread properly, since her hands were backward, palms facing the opposite way from how they should.

"Hello, dear child," Wander said in a voice that hummed like a tuning fork. She finished spinning the thread, holding it looped around one hand, and rose. "Come help me with this, will you?"

Eleanor glanced at Jack, who gave her an encouraging nod. She stepped forward, uncertain what kind of help Wander could mean. The woman handed her the skein of moonlight-thread. It was cool and slippery, and Eleanor fumbled to get a good hold on it.

Wander reached into the pocket of her gown, the color of dusk, and drew out a little leather case that held a long wooden needle. She threaded the end of the moonlight through it and motioned to Eleanor to follow her, five steps out from the orchard. Humming once again, she started to move the needle back and forth, as if sewing fabric. The thread followed, stitches appearing in the air where the needle passed, though there was nothing to hold them up. Eleanor watched in wordless wonder.

"Traveling through the Wending's roads is a delicate business," Wander said. When she had appeared four days ago, it had been at the end of a road that appeared out of nowhere, running straight through Pip's house. "It sometimes leaves a tear. And if you don't mend it quickly, you're likely to incur the anger of the Wending's guardians."

"Guardians?" Eleanor asked, alarmed. "What kind of guardians?"

"Those ones," Wander said calmly, gesturing, as a low growl sounded to the left.

Eleanor turned with a sinking feeling in the pit of her stomach.

Two

Two lithe dogs with pointed muzzles stood near the edge of the pine forest that surrounded the town of Eden Eld. One of them was bone white with long, silky fur. The other was pitch-black, with short fur that made it look like a silhouette against the forest. They sniffed the air, eyes fixed on Jack, Wander, and Eleanor.

Wander finished sewing up the air and snipped the end of the thread with a pair of tiny silver scissors. "There we go," she said loudly, as if to the hounds. "No damage done."

The two hounds paced forward, one going left and the other right to make a wide circle around the three humans. The black one bared gleaming teeth. The white one growled deep in its chest.

"You aren't welcome on our roads," the white one said, in an echoing voice. It was feminine, with a ragged, toothy edge.

"They aren't for you to travel," the black one added, her voice lower. It sounded like it was coming from a dark cavern far underground. They paused at exactly the same moment, one paw raised, ears pricked forward. Their eyes were white blazes of light. Jack stepped back so that he was right next to Eleanor, his arm out as if to shield her.

"Rag-a-bone, Shatterblack, I go where I will and I do not answer to you or your mistress," Wander said. She flicked her hand. The shimmering shards around her surged toward the dark-furred dog—Shatterblack—who leaped back as if afraid to be touched.

"Eleanor, stay behind me," Jack said.

The hounds surged forward before the last word left his lips. They arced through the air.

"Run!" Jack yelled to Eleanor.

Eleanor wanted to fight, but she didn't have special abilities or weapons or even an ounce of athletic talent that might make a difference. So she ran, dashing back toward the house. She could find something inside to help. She could—

Something slammed into her back, taking her down to the ground. Rag-a-bone, teeth snapping. Eleanor screamed and twisted onto her back, throwing her hands up to protect herself.

The moonlight thread she still held whipped up, smacking Rag-a-bone across her long muzzle. There was a pop and a sizzle. Rag-a-bone howled. Then Jack was there, grabbing hold of Rag-a-bone's scruff and tossing her away. She scrambled to her feet growling, but Eleanor whipped the end of the moonlight thread toward her again and she dodged back with a snarl.

Wander's glittering stars seethed around Eleanor and Jack, a threatening cloud, and Wander herself strode into view with a thread of moonlight snapping like a whip in her hand. "The way is mended. Go back to your mistress and bother us no more," she said.

They looked at each other. "Stay out of the Wending ways," Shatterblack growled.

"We would hate to have to hunt you," Rag-a-bone added, tilting her muzzle so her teeth glinted in the moonlight.

"No, we wouldn't," Shatterblack said, sounding puzzled. "We would enjoy it very much."

Rag-a-bone gave the other hound a withering look, then flicked her tail and streaked away into the night. Shatterblack was quick on her heels—and then both were gone.

"What *has* gotten into them?" Wander mused. She was panting a little, and long strands of hair hung loose around her face. The gleaming motes around her danced in quick, jerky movements. Some of them had turned crimson, and without thinking Eleanor put her hand out curiously to touch one. It bounced off the tip of her middle finger. Eleanor yelped and snatched her hand back; a tiny drop of blood welled where it had touched her.

"They're glass?" she said. What she'd taken for magical little stars, she saw, were fragments of shattered glass. Wander flicked her hand, and the cloud rose into the air above her.

"My apologies. I should have warned you not to touch them," Wander said, getting her breath back. "Now. What were we talking about?"

"How about the talking dogs that tried to eat us?" Eleanor suggested.

"Umbral hounds," Jack said, sounding troubled. "They're crossroads guardians. They're not normally aggressive unless you've done something to damage the paths between worlds."

"They have a new mistress. They've been cranky," Wander said dismissively. "They won't bother us again tonight, I think."

"I would still feel better if we were safely inside," Jack said.

Wander arched an eyebrow. "The umbral hounds don't stop for doors and locks, old friend."

"Bartimaeus Ashford built this house. Even you couldn't get through the protections he put on it without being invited," Jack replied, and Wander eyed the house with new interest.

"Well, then. Shall we?" Wander said. She drifted inside, her glass motes following.

Eleanor started to follow, but Jack caught her arm.

"Are you all right?" he asked, his voice gruff with concern.

"Just some dirt and a bruise or two," she assured him. She'd spent so much time fantasizing about having her dad in her life. Now she had him, and she didn't know how to feel. Eleanor was cursed and *probably* doomed. He was just one more person she was inevitably going to lose.

She followed Wander's faintly glowing footsteps through the house, into the Great Room, and up the stairs hidden at the back of the fireplace. At the top of the stairs was a seemingly solid wall that concealed a secret door. Eleanor pushed it open and entered, Jack right behind her.

The room beyond was long—far too long to have actually fit into the space between the fireplace and the rest of the house—and filled with shelves and display cases containing strange and magical objects collected by Bartimaeus Ashford, the man who'd built the house. Wander had bent over one of the display cases and was examining a deck of fortune-telling cards.

"Wander?" Eleanor said. Wander straightened up with a little distracted *hmm* and looked back at her, blinking.

"What is it, dear?" Wander asked.

"Wasn't there something you wanted to tell me? I mean, before the hounds attacked us."

"Quite possibly," Wander agreed, nodding. Jack sighed. It was a sigh that suggested this was not at all unusual for Wander. "We should gather your friends, and I will tell you all at once," Wander continued. "The warrior, and the clever one who speaks very quickly?"

"Otto," Eleanor said. "The thing is, it's already after nine, and tomorrow is a school day, so there's no way their parents are going to let them go out right now."

"That is no obstacle, so long as you grant me permission," Wander said.

"Permission?" Eleanor echoed, and then remembered what Jack had said about the house's protections. "Sure, you have permission to do . . . whatever you're doing."

"Wonderful," Wander said. She rose and raised her hands, pressing her fingertips together, and then swept them outward. Two shimmering vertical lines appeared to either side of her.

Then they split, parting like curtains. Beyond them lay two very familiar bedrooms.

Pip was lying on her bed, watching a video on her phone. She sat up abruptly when she spotted Wander, and suddenly Gloaming—the magical sword she'd inherited from Jack—appeared in her hand. Pip had pale skin, a glorious set of freckles, and red hair that had gotten particularly fiery since the Prime Story had chosen her. She'd gotten taller, too, and more muscular. Her eyes were a pure, flat gray: the surest sign that the Prime Story had taken hold.

Through the opposite wall, Otto looked up from his desk, which was stacked high with school textbooks and leather-bound tomes of magic, and gaped. His tight curls were sticking out around his headphones. He had warm brown skin and rich brown eyes—but as the light flashed across those eyes, Eleanor thought for a moment they might be gray instead.

No. She had to be wrong about that. He couldn't be a Story, too.

"Please. Join us," Wander said, beckoning to them.

Otto cautiously removed his headphones. Pip slid off the bed and walked to what must have been the wall of her bedroom, right on the other side of the shimmering portal. She eyed it suspiciously. "How are you doing this?" she asked.

"I am the world-walker. I can always find my friends," Wander said.

"Are we friends?" Otto asked, creeping forward.

"I should hope so," Wander replied.

"She just wants to talk to us," Eleanor added, staring in wonder between the two portals. Jack was good at swinging a sword and stuff, and the hedgewitch had helped them out with a magical ritual this past spring, but this was *incredible.*

Pip was the first to step forward. "You should text first next time. You're lucky I'm wearing pants," she noted casually as she passed through the portal.

Otto took his time, like he wanted to savor the experience, sticking his fingers through first and giving them a good wiggle before holding his breath and easing his way across. The bright edges of the portals collapsed behind the two of them, leaving only the solid walls of the storeroom once more. Otto whistled, impressed.

"Is this about that thing you mentioned when you got here?" Pip asked, straight to business. "The Wending?"

"Indeed. The Wending," Wander said with a dramatic pause, "is open."

"Okay," Pip said, her impatience putting brambles in her words. "But what *is* the Wending?"

"Didn't I tell you?" Wander said. They all shook their heads. "The Wending is how Mr. January's sister is planning to capture you."

Three

"The Wending isn't a *thing* or a *place.* It's the roads between worlds," Wander explained. "It connects all the worlds that are, that were, and that will be. Even some that *might* have been. You could step through the Wending and into ancient Greece, or the Library of Endersea, or the halls of Atlantis."

"Atlantis is real?" Otto asked.

Wander smiled. "No, but it *might* have been, and so the Wending can take you there. My abilities allow me to open doorways between worlds that are close to each other—the ones pressed up against each other's borders. But if you know how to navigate the Wending, you can enter any world you wish."

"And what does this have to do with Mr. January's sister?" Eleanor asked.

Wander looked grim. "The man you know as Mr. January comes from a place called the Pallid Kingdom. A horrible place, with a king and queen intent on devouring all the good of every world. So wicked were they that long ago, their world was cut off from all the rest. But their children were trapped outside the Pallid Kingdom. They have been trying to get back and free their parents ever since."

Eleanor nodded. They knew this, or at least bits and pieces of it.

"The youngest of the siblings studied the ways between worlds, hoping she could find a way to open the path back to the Pallid Kingdom directly. Her search brought her to the Wending—and at last, recently, she became its mistress. She commands the umbral hounds, and she controls the Wending's many roads."

"So why doesn't she just use it to get home?" Eleanor asked.

"The way to the Pallid Kingdom she seeks is barred. Even the Wending can't reach it—not without breaking reality entirely. Your mother knows more about the Wending, Eleanor, but I have been unable to contact her."

Eleanor flinched. Her mother had been missing now for al most a year, ever since their house burned down with Eleanor in it. At first, Eleanor had thought her mother set the fire and abandoned her. Then she found out that her mother had to run away because an evil society of the descendants of Eden Eld's founders was after her. And last spring, she'd discovered that her mother had been chosen by the hedgewitch, one of the Prime Stories, before Eleanor was even born. Her mother had tried to resist the story as long as she could, but eventually it took her over and erased the person she'd been before. When Eleanor had seen her a few months ago, she hadn't even remembered Eleanor.

"Okay, so sister number two is the queen of the Wending, or whatever," Pip said. "What does it mean that it's open?"

"Most of the time, the Wending is impossible to access," Wander said. "If its mistress has opened it, it's because she needs to use it. The timing suggests that you are the reason for that."

"The clock in the hall isn't ticking. Or running backward," Eleanor said. She checked every day. When Mr. January and Mrs. Prosper came after them, the clock warned them, but it had been quiet for months.

"So maybe we still have some time," Otto said, but he looked as uneasy as Eleanor felt. "What do you think she's going to try to do? Bring some big nasty monster from another world?"

"Monsters aren't a problem," Pip said, tapping a finger against Gloaming's hilt.

"I dunno, I have a pretty big problem with monsters," Otto muttered.

Eleanor didn't reply, lost in thought. The People Who Look Away—Mr. January, Mrs. Prosper, and their sister—each had a special day they claimed as their own. For Mr. January, it was Halloween. For Mrs. Prosper, it was the spring equinox. They'd considered everything from the summer solstice to National Ice Cream Day as dates of interest for the final sister. Pip had also suggested the last day of school, which was a couple weeks away, but Eleanor had tactfully pointed out that the Eden Eld

Academy academic calendar probably didn't have mystical significance.

"The summer solstice is in three weeks," she said.

"The timing seems about right," Otto said, following her train of thought.

"And National Ice Cream Day doesn't have quite the right mystical ring to it," Pip agreed. "Three weeks, huh? Well, it's more warning than we've had so far."

"Wander. If I could speak to you for a moment in private," Jack said. She nodded and rose from her spot, and the two of them drew off to the side as Jack spoke in low, serious tones.

Pip glanced at Otto and bit her lip. He met her eyes, and just like Jenny and Ben had, they seemed to be holding a whole conversation. Pip widened her eyes meaningfully. Otto tilted his head toward Eleanor. Pip scowled. They had been best friends since they were babies, and they were always doing this.

"What is it?" Eleanor asked, sighing.

"It's about the Stories," Otto said. He wetted his lips nervously. "Eleanor, I think the other Stories might be . . . *noticing* us."

"What do you mean?" Eleanor asked, her voice hoarse. She hadn't told him about his eyes—about how they'd been flashing gray since they'd escaped from Mrs. Prosper. Ever since Otto had performed a ritual given to them by the hedgewitch—exactly the sort of thing the Stories might be drawn to.

He took a deep breath. "Eleanor, we haven't told you because we didn't want to freak you out until we were sure. But I saw something after we got back from the Wickerwood, and I keep seeing it. Pip has, too."

"Your eyes," Eleanor whispered. "They're turning gray."

They stared at her. "What?" Otto said.

"That's not what you were going to say?" she asked him, panicky.

"No, I . . ." He swallowed. "My eyes are turning gray?" His voice was tight and fearful.

Pip stared at him. "Oh no," she said, looking stricken. "I didn't see."

Eleanor nodded, tears pricking her eyes. She shouldn't have kept it a secret. She just wanted it not to be true. "But if that's not what you were going to tell me—" she started.

Pip swallowed. "We weren't going to tell you that Otto's eyes were turning gray."

Eleanor felt something squeeze behind her ribs, like a knot pulling tight.

"We were going to tell you that yours are."

Four

The next morning, Eleanor wedged herself into the back seat of the bus and wrapped her arms around her backpack. At the next stop, Otto plopped down next to her, looking frazzled, with his dress shirt untucked from his slacks and his tie loose around his neck.

"Hey," he said.

"Hey," she answered. They looked at each other glumly. The bus trundled along—then slowed and stopped, pausing at a stop sign.

"Why are we stopping?" Otto asked.

"There shouldn't be a stop sign here, should there?" Eleanor replied, peering out the window. Were they going a different way?

This was the right street, with the U-pick strawberry farm on the left and the pasture of fat, lazy goats on the right. The road intersecting it, though, had never been there before.

It looked in every way like a normal road. The asphalt was the same gray as the street they were on, and it neatly divided the strawberry fields as if it had always been that way. The only thing wrong about it was that it existed at all.

"I'm not imagining things, right? That road wasn't there on Friday?" Otto whispered. Eleanor nodded. She looked at the bus driver, who had started forward again. Eleanor could see the woman's reflection in the rearview mirror, an expression of utter bafflement on her face. As soon as they picked up speed, though, her expression smoothed. She reached over to turn on the radio, cranking Taylor Swift as loud as she would go.

Eleanor twisted to watch the strange road. She kept her eyes fixed on it, waiting for it to shimmer and vanish or to sprout teeth or something equally horrific, but it just stayed a road, until she couldn't see it anymore.

"The Wending?" Otto whispered.

Eleanor pulled her journal out of her backpack and opened it to a page titled *Possible Signs of Wrong Things, Mr. January, Etc.* Most of the items on the list had been crossed off or were labeled "resolved" or "harmless" or "avoid."

Roads that shouldn't be there, she wrote at the bottom of the list, and strained to hear the sound of a ticking clock—the surefire sign of approaching trouble in the past. But there was only the rumbling of the bus and the nervous tapping of Otto's fingers against the vinyl seat.

PIP WAS WAITING for them near the front steps, and she looked just as tired as they did. She had dark shadows under her eyes and her hair was a helpless tangle. She yawned and waved blearily to them as they approached.

They told her about the extra road as they meandered down the hall. They didn't have classes all together until the afternoon, which meant as soon as the bell rang, they'd be split up. "So nobody hears the clock?" Eleanor finished.

"Not a tick or a tock," Pip said. She peered at the two of them. "No gray eyes today. That's something."

"How long will that last, though?" Otto asked. "You're forgetting more things, too."

Pip shrugged. "Nothing important. Just kid stuff."

Otto's expression was hurt, but he looked away as if to hide it from Pip. Otto and Pip had been best friends all their lives. "Kid stuff" meant memories of their childhood together. Pip was acting like it didn't matter at all.

The bell rang, giving them five minutes' warning to get to class. They parted reluctantly, agreeing to meet up at lunch like they always did, and Eleanor headed for science class and slouched her way over to the table she shared with her lab partner, Katie Rhodes, a girl with a cheery round face and blond hair that always managed to look mussed.

At the next table over, Andy Park sat with his best friend, Ryan Wylie. Andy caught Eleanor's gaze and gave her a friendly wave. Eleanor looked away quickly, the memory of last night's cocoa debacle making her cheeks hot, and slid into her chair as casually as she could.

"Do you like Andy?" Katie asked, and Eleanor almost squawked.

"Why would you ask that?" she demanded. Katie blinked rapidly, holding up a Starburst.

"Because I have extra?" she said meekly.

"Do I like *candy*," Eleanor repeated, blushing even harder. *It could be worse,* she thought. She could actually have a crush on Andy, and then this would be *mortifying*. Since she didn't have a crush on anyone, it was totally fine, really.

Katie blinked some more. "*Do* you like Andy?" she whispered, connecting the dots between Eleanor's embarrassment and the Starburst.

"No," Eleanor said a bit too loudly. Katie stifled a laugh as Andy and Ryan glanced over.

"I kind of thought you liked Mabel," Katie confessed, and Eleanor groaned. Katie laughed good-naturedly as Eleanor buried her head in her arms on the table. "It's okay, I won't tell anyone. And I promise not to bring maple cookies next time."

There was nothing *to* tell, Eleanor wanted to say. There was absolutely no point figuring out who she liked if she was never going to get to go on a date or have a first kiss or even hold hands under the table, was there? So she didn't know if she liked Andy or Mabel or even whether she liked girls or boys or both or neither.

Katie poked her shoulder. "Sorry. I didn't mean to embarrass you," she said.

"It's fine," Eleanor said into the tabletop.

Eleanor had been Katie's lab partner all semester. She always felt kind of bad, because Katie was really nice and clearly wanted to be friends, but Eleanor just didn't have room for the regular kind of friends. The kind you went to the movies and played board games with, instead of researching curses and experimenting with magical concoctions. The kind where you wrote *Have a nice summer* in their yearbook, instead of *Hope we're still alive in the fall hahaha.*

The bell to start class rang, and Mr. Crouch moved to the front of the room, clasping his hands in excited anticipation. "Today is an *amazing* day," he declared. Then he paused. "Actually, today isn't the amazing day. Today is the day we get *ready* for the amazing day. *Saturday* will be amazing," he said, and looked at them, grinning, as if waiting for them to burst into spontaneous applause.

Eleanor put up a tentative hand. "Mr. Crouch? Why is Saturday amazing?" she asked.

"Oh!" he said. "Sorry, I'm getting ahead of myself. Or possibly behind. On Saturday morning, we are going to be witnesses to a rare event: a total eclipse. Eden Eld will be directly in the path of totality, meaning that for a few wondrous moments, the moon will completely cover the sun. Day will turn to night."

Eleanor's jaw dropped. An eclipse.

A time when day and night switched places.

A *magical* time.

It was exactly the sort of thing the People Who Look Away adored, and Eleanor and the others had missed it.

"Today, we're going to make pinhole cameras," Mr. Crouch said. "They'll allow you to observe the eclipse safely, without damaging your eyes. I'd like you all to use your cameras this Saturday and record your observations."

There were a few groans—Saturday homework? Eleanor just sat, still and tense, trying to breathe slowly so her pulse wouldn't race.

If they were wrong and the People Who Look Away were coming for them during the eclipse, not the solstice, they had a whole *week* less than they'd thought to prepare.

"If at all possible, I'd like you to pair up with your lab partners to take your observations," Mr. Crouch was saying.

Katie nudged Eleanor's shoulder. "Want to come over to my place Saturday?"

Eleanor winced. "I'm not sure. I might have other plans," she hedged. Katie's face fell. "But maybe," she added quickly, feeling bad, and Katie perked back up.

"Now, because of our position, totality—when the moon is fully covering the sun—will last only a few minutes, so you all need to be ready well before then," Mr. Crouch went on.

Oh, we'll be ready, Eleanor thought with determination. But even if she couldn't hear it, she could now feel the ticking of a clock. Time was running out.

KATIE KEPT UP a pleasant stream of conversation the whole time they made their camera, and Eleanor found herself grateful for the distraction. Katie was really very nice, if a bit boring, and Eleanor couldn't exactly fault her for that given that Eleanor's definition of "interesting" usually involved magic and mortal peril. Boring was good, actually. With Katie she could *almost* pretend she was a normal teenager with normal teenager problems.

They left class together, Katie still chattering about nothing in particular. Eleanor had math class next. She started to turn the corner—then stopped dead. She'd turned too soon. This wasn't the hall to math class. There were red lockers lining the walls and the maroon-and-white floor tiles like the rest of the school, but there shouldn't have been a hall there at all—this should have been Mr. Ryland's social studies room.

Through the doors along the hall, students sat in orderly rows, staring forward with their hands on their laps. Their shoulders didn't seem shaped right—too soft and smooth. And Eleanor couldn't read the teachers' names on the doors or the posters on the walls. It wasn't that they were blurry—it was more like trying to read in a dream, the words refusing to surrender their meaning no matter how hard you stared at them.

She swallowed. She tried to turn away only to find that she couldn't; her right foot was in the hallway already. It was stuck. She gritted her teeth and hauled backward, but instead her body twitched forward. Her left foot lifted up, stepping out.

Katie grabbed her elbow and yanked her backward, and Eleanor yelped. She stumbled back into Katie, who stumbled back into a passing sixth-grader, who stumbled into the lockers, dropping his books.

"Oh my gosh, I'm sorry!" Katie said, and she and Eleanor hastily picked up the dropped books, straightened the dazed-looking sixth-grader's jacket, and sent him on his way. By the time they were done, the strange hallway had vanished, and Mr. Ryland's classroom was back where it belonged. Eleanor stared at it. She looked sideways at it—sometimes you could see Wrong Things better out of the corner of your eye. Mr. Ryland's room remained.

Eleanor looked at Katie, whose cheeks were flushed but who did not look like someone who had just witnessed the impossible. "Did you see . . ." she started.

Katie's eyes got a blank look that Eleanor knew well. It was the look of someone forgetting what they'd just seen. "You almost went into the wrong class," she said, and giggled.

"Thanks for pulling me back," Eleanor said with feeling. Katie gave her a confused look.

Eleanor didn't want to know what would have happened if she'd kept walking down that hallway. The rest of the way to math class, she checked every turn carefully before she stepped around the corner. No more phantom hallways appeared, but when she sat down at her desk, she opened her journal to the page where she'd written *Roads that shouldn't be there* and underlined it three times.

Five

Jenny and Ben were used to seeing Otto and Pip pile off the bus after Eleanor, and Ben already had snacks laid out for them.

"Hey, kids!" he said as they ran into the kitchen, dumping their backpacks and snatching up the tray of cheese and crackers. "Bye, kids!"

"Thanks, Uncle Ben," Eleanor said over her shoulder, and bolted after Pip and Otto. They paused only long enough to make sure the coast was clear before heading up the fireplace steps and into the secret room.

Wander and Jack were already inside. Jack had fetched some chairs from the house, along with a card table. He was seated with his reading glasses on, paging through a textbook called *Introduction to Internet Basics*. He was still working on getting up-to date on modern life. Wander was standing at the rear of the room, where a round mirror looked out over an ever-shifting landscape. When the trio entered, she turned toward them with her usual dreamy smile.

"You're back," she said in delighted surprise, as if she'd had no idea they were coming. Jack stifled a sigh as he set his book down and tucked his glasses into his shirt pocket.

"Yeah, we're back, and we've got *problems*," Pip said. She set her tray of snacks down on the card table and flopped into the chair. Eleanor and Otto took seats as well, helping themselves to crackers.

"What sort of problems?" Wander asked, concern creasing her brow.

"Today on the way to school there was a road that wasn't there yesterday, and at school there was a hallway that didn't exist, and I think it might have tried to eat me," Eleanor said.

"We think maybe that's the third sibling's plan," Otto said. "Trap us on a road somehow."

Wander tapped her finger against her lips, considering. "It's also possible that a predatory pathway followed me. Some roads are hungrier than others. If anyone ever tells you they can show you the way to Ys, trust me, run the other way."

"That's not all," Eleanor said. "It turns out there's an eclipse on Saturday. A total eclipse."

"I can't believe I missed it," Otto said, looking dejected.

"We've had a lot to keep track of," Pip reassured him, slinging an arm around his shoulders. "And I'm still not convinced. It's not a day, like the others. It's more of an . . . an event. Didn't Mr. Crouch say it only lasts a few minutes?"

"That could be a good thing," Eleanor said. "Only a few minutes of danger."

"Or a very bad thing. Only a few minutes to get *out* of danger," Otto countered. He looked at the adults. "What do you think? Eclipse, or solstice?"

Wander pursed her lips. "Were I to pick the one more suited to the mistress of the Wending, I would say the eclipse. But it is impossible to be certain."

"We'll be wary, regardless," Jack pledged.

"Yeah, don't go down any weird roads," Pip suggested. "And we should all meet up that morning. Make sure we're all together in case something goes down."

"I'll have to ditch my lab partner first," Otto said. "She sort of invited herself over to my house already."

"I already told mine I was doing it with you guys," Pip said with a shrug.

Eleanor thought of Katie and felt a pang of guilt. She really did wish she could be a better friend—but what was the point, anyway? She was probably going to get turned into a key, and she couldn't exactly show up for movie night *then*. "We'll meet up here," she said firmly. "Whatever the People Who Look Away are trying to throw at us, we can handle it."

"Indeed. To that end, I have prepared lists of supplies to have ready before the fateful day," Jack intoned, holding out three pages of notebook paper covered in his scrawling handwriting.

Pip picked one up and snorted. "Sunscreen? You're such a *dad*." She rolled her eyes. Jack struggled to hide a pleased smile, and Eleanor pressed her lips together, stifling a laugh.

"This is a terrible list," Pip went on, shaking her head. "Not nearly enough snacks. Or weaponry." She pulled a pen out of her back pocket and began making changes.

Eleanor looked down the list. Jack had suggested books, potions, flashlights, rope, and, despite Pip's objections, a startling array of sharp objects. He'd even put life jackets on the list. It was enough to fill the whole garage. "This is a lot," she noted delicately.

Jack looked troubled. "We don't know what to expect. I tried to prepare for every eventuality," he said.

A strange feeling shimmered and shuddered through Eleanor. Words seemed to rise to her tongue without her thinking of them first, and when she spoke her voice didn't sound quite like her own. "Then we undertake the task with nothing but our wits, our courage, and one another," she said.

Otto and Pip stilled. Jack stared openly. "Isn't that a line from *Tales of the Gray*?" Otto asked uncertainly.

"I . . . I don't know," Eleanor said, but she knew perfectly well it was.

They were the words the girl with backward hands spoke in the tale of *Tatterskin*. That *Wander* had spoken, Eleanor realized with a start.

As if Wander's tale was seeping into her mind, bit by bit.

OUTSIDE HER ROOM that night, she paused to look at the grandfather clock that stood opposite her door. It was a tall clock, the case carved from dark oak and the face the color of pearl. The hands of the clock ran backward, counting from twelve to eleven to ten to nine. Thirteen keys were painted around the numbers, the last one faint as if almost rubbed away. Each of those keys represented a trio of children stolen from Eden Eld by the People Who Look Away. The last key was hers—hers, and Pip's, and Otto's.

The clock had warned them before, its ticking following them wherever they went. She could hear the steady *tick-tock-tick* as she stood here in the hall, but downstairs there had been no hint of it. *Not yet,* she thought. They were safe for now.

That night, Eleanor dreamed again of Rag-a-bone and Shatterblack, their lolling pink tongues and snapping white teeth. But this time, as their hot breath panted on the back of her legs, she was suddenly lifted out of the dream by a soft voice.

"Eleanor."

She startled awake as Wander's fingertips brushed her brow. The woman bent over her, glass shards drifting like dust caught in a beam of sunlight. Eleanor sat up, sitting back against the headboard. "I was dreaming about the hounds," she said.

"I know." Wander sat on the end of the bed. "They can't harm you in your dreams, but they can keep you from sleep.

Here." She twisted her fingers, and a loop of shining silver thread appeared, braided into a bracelet. She settled it around Eleanor's wrist. "That will keep your dreams protected."

Eleanor ran her fingers along the bumps of the braided thread, and the bracelet made a sound like a sigh, settling snugly against her skin.

"Eleanor. I think you and I need to talk," Wander said quietly.

Eleanor's lip began to quiver. She bunched her hands into fists and took a sharp breath through her nose. "Otto and I—we're becoming Stories, aren't we?" she asked.

"It is not a certain thing for you, yet. Not as it was with Pip. Do not despair."

"Otto's Story is the hedgewitch, right?" Eleanor asked. "The hedgewitch is all about knowledge and naming things and learning, and that's totally Otto. So that leaves the world-walker. But why would it want *me*? I'm nothing special."

"You are the daughter of two Stories. That is a very rare thing. One that makes you more suited to slipping between worlds."

Eleanor looked over at *Thirteen Tales of the Gray*, which sat in its customary place on her bedside. "In the book, it says that the girl with backward hands was the daughter of a princess who was taken by Mr. January," she said. "It's implied that—I mean, it seems like Mr. January is—I mean . . ." She trailed off, not sure how to ask such an awkward question.

"The tale implies that the girl with backward hands is the daughter of Mr. January and the stolen princess," Wander said with a wry twist of her lips. "I promise you, I am not Mr. January's child. Bartimaeus Ashford took significant liberties when he recorded those stories."

Eleanor nodded. The stories had hints of truth in them, but rarely stated things outright.

Wander picked up *Thirteen Tales*, paging through it with her spidery hands. Her fingernail ran down the title page, rasping softly against the paper, and then she flipped ahead. She held the book out for Eleanor to see. "This is my story. Or what little I remembered of it, embellished by Bartimaeus's imagination."

"*The Glass-Heart Girl*?" Eleanor asked, seeing what story it was open to. Wander nodded, and Eleanor read aloud the familiar words.

> *Once upon a time in a kingdom of magic, a princess was born with a heart of glass. Her glass heart beat normally, but each time she tightened her fists and wailed, tiny cracks appeared on its surface. The king and queen warned their daughter as she grew: Do not be moved to anger. Do not weep with sorrow. Do not quail with fear. Most of all, do not love: for however strong your love, sooner or later, your heart will break. And while any other broken heart might mend, a glass heart could only shatter.*

The princess obeyed her parents. She knew neither joy nor sorrow, neither rage nor relief, and above all she resisted the lure of love. Until one day a knight came to the kingdom, fair of hair and blue of eye. From the moment she saw him, her glass heart was filled with love.

Eleanor paused in her reading, her fingers trailing under the words. "How much of it is true?" she asked.

"I don't remember anymore," Wander said. Her fingers traced the illustration on the opposite page: a princess extending her hand to a dashing knight, clad in armor. He had pale hair and sharp good looks, and his eyes gazed upon the princess with adoration. "Perhaps the true story still exists in the Library of Endersea—it is said its shelves contain every story from every world. But it is lost to me forever."

"In the book, she falls in love, but the knight dies," Eleanor said. "Her heart breaks into a thousand pieces. She dies, too." It was the saddest story in the book.

"I didn't die," Wander said quietly. "But it hurt so much I wished I had. That's the only part I remember. The pain of it. You need to guard your heart, as I did not. Promise me that."

She touched her fingertips to Eleanor's chin, tilting it up. Her eyes glinted with reflected moonlight—and so did the shards of glass that danced and swayed around her. *Her heart*, Eleanor thought. It was with her still.

"I promise," she whispered, and Wander nodded, satisfied.

"Sleep well," she said. "The hounds won't trouble you."

Eleanor lay back down as Wander left, closing the door behind her. But even knowing the hounds would not plague her dreams, she couldn't sleep. She stared at the ceiling instead, and thought of Jenny and Ben and baby Naomi, and of her parents, and crushes, and all of the things that felt even a little like love.

Wander was right. She couldn't worry about those things right now. She needed to be strong. Strong, but cold and clear as glass.

Six

The morning of the eclipse was warm, with not a cloud in the sky. Eleanor sat on the front porch, where she'd been since before sunrise, unable to sleep. The perfect summer day, and Eleanor couldn't appreciate one bit of it. The clock in the hall had been silent all week. They had seen more strange roads around town, but no amount of watching them had yielded any clues, and they hadn't found answers in Bartimaeus Ashford's books or anywhere else.

The door opened. Jack stepped out, hands in his pockets. "The clock is running backward as always," he said. "Can you hear it?"

Eleanor shook her head.

"Then perhaps the eclipse is unrelated," Jack said. "It's the solstice after all."

"I'm not going to relax until the eclipse is over, whatever the clock says," Eleanor replied.

Eleanor's phone chimed in her pocket. **On my way over,** Otto texted.

See you soon, she sent back. Pip didn't reply. She lived farther away, but she was also a lot harder to wake up in the morning, so Eleanor tried not to feel too nervous about the fact that she hadn't checked in. She'd be here.

Jenny was calling from the kitchen.

"Shall we?" Jack asked.

In the kitchen, Jenny was making a giant pile of waffles. Eleanor looked at the array of fruits and berries and syrups and wished she had even a little bit of an appetite.

"I hope you're hungry," Jenny said.

"Ravenous," said Jack, who had a serious sweet tooth.

Eleanor *hmm*-ed. Jenny gave her a hard look over her shoulder. "You're always going around with the weight of the world on your shoulders, Eleanor. And I get it. But don't forget to enjoy some waffles now and then, too."

Behind Eleanor, the doorbell rang. Otto already? "I'll get it," she said quickly, and hurried back through the hallway before Jenny could expand on her pep talk.

Eleanor opened the door, expecting to find Otto—or even Pip—and blinked in confusion to discover Katie standing on the welcome mat, her pinhole camera carefully cradled in her arms and a cheerful smile rounding her cheeks.

"Good morning!" she chirped. "I know I'm early but I'm just really, really excited."

Eleanor stared at her. "I—but we—"

"Katie! Good, you made it in time for waffles," Jenny said, popping out from the kitchen. Jack followed behind, casting a questioning look between Katie and Eleanor.

"I love waffles," Katie declared, stepping in past Eleanor.

"You knew she was coming?" Eleanor asked.

"Of course. Her mom called to make sure we were okay to host yesterday," Jenny said, giving Eleanor a puzzled frown.

"Right. Of course," Eleanor said, mentally cursing herself. Okay, maybe she hadn't gotten around to telling Katie she couldn't come over—not when she didn't have a good excuse. Katie would just think she didn't want to be friends.

Katie traipsed cheerfully into the kitchen for waffles. Jack dropped his voice as he spoke to Eleanor. "This was not part of the plan."

"I know, I know," Eleanor told him. "But I can't tell her to leave now. There's no way to do it that isn't completely awful."

"Being devoured by umbral hounds would be significantly more awful," Jack pointed out, raising an eyebrow. Eleanor slumped. Maybe this was what Wander was talking about, when she said to guard your heart. *Cold as glass*, Eleanor thought. *Do what has to be done.*

Eleanor took a deep breath and walked into the kitchen. Katie was sitting at the table already, piling up her plate with waffles. The pinhole camera sat on the table beside her. Eleanor paused in the doorway. She looked back at Jack, who gave her a nod.

"Katie, I'm sorry, but we can't do our observations together," she said.

Jenny glanced up sharply from where she was tending the waffle iron. Katie looked startled. "Why not?" she asked.

Cold as glass, Eleanor thought. "Pip and Otto and I are doing it together," she said. "Just the three of us." She said it firmly, and she didn't need to say anything else—she knew her meaning was clear. Just us, and not you. Because you aren't our friend.

"Eleanor," Jenny said in a dangerous tone, but Katie was already slipping from her seat, her cheeks beet red.

"Oh," she said, looking down at her feet. "I'm sorry. I didn't know. I'll go."

"You don't have to go anywhere," Jenny said, her expression furious. Eleanor flinched and looked away. Jenny thought she was awful. But she had to do this. She had to.

"I'd rather go," Katie said. "I'm just going to go call my mom."

Before Jenny could stop her, she stumbled past Eleanor into the hall. Eleanor tried not to notice that there were tears in her eyes, or that the front door slammed loudly on her way out.

"Eleanor Barton, what *exactly* was that about?" Jenny demanded, a hand on her hip. "Is this what you're going to be like now that you're a teenager? Some kind of mean girl?"

Eleanor looked helplessly back at Jack, but he looked as uncomfortable as she felt. She looked back at the abandoned plate of waffles. Katie hadn't even had time to add the syrup. Her pinhole camera sat next to the plate, forgotten.

"Oh no," Eleanor said. She hurried forward to grab it. "She's going to need this. I'll just . . ." Ducking under Jenny's steely glare, she hurried out of the kitchen. She felt like the worst person in the world. The least she could do was give Katie her camera back.

She stepped out onto the porch. Her phone was chiming. She pulled it out and glanced down at it as she walked.

Slight complication, have to deal with something, Pip had written.

Guys I glbklrbr, read a message from Otto. Eleanor frowned at the key-smash, but didn't have time to ask him what he meant. She stepped off the porch and glanced up toward Katie, who had her phone to her ear and was walking up the path toward the driveway.

A path that forked, when it had never forked before. One fork of the walkway led to the driveway just like it was supposed to, but the other bent sharply away, slithering off into the grass where there had never been a walkway before.

"Katie, look out!" Eleanor cried. She ran forward, dropping the pinhole camera, but Katie had already stepped out onto the wrong path. The one that shouldn't exist. She stopped, stock-still, as if her feet were rooted in place. And then she started forward again. "Katie, stop!" Eleanor said, rushing up to the edge of where the paths split.

"I can't," Katie wailed. She twisted, looking over her shoulder. She seemed to strain—and her foot moved forward, one step farther along the road. "Eleanor, what's happening?"

"Hold on." Eleanor reached out to try to snatch her arm. Eleanor's fingers clamped around Katie's hand, and she let out a cry of triumph—and then Katie jerked forward another step, taking Eleanor with her.

Eleanor's free hand pinwheeled, trying to get her balance, but it was no use. Her foot hit the false path, and then she was lurching forward, her feet carrying her along behind Katie. Katie craned her neck to look back, face stricken with terror.

"What's happening?" she cried.

"I don't know," Eleanor said. "But it's going to be okay. I promise."

They walked at a rapid clip. The path wrapped behind the house, to the orchard, and wriggled between the trees, which stretched farther than they should have with no end in sight.

Eleanor looked desperately at her phone. No signal. Her skin crawled with a strange sensation. She felt like she was brushing through cobwebs.

"E-E-Eleanor?" Katie said, teeth chattering with fear. "Where are we going?"

"I don't know," Eleanor said. They were heading farther and farther from the house—and the sky was starting to grow dim. She put on a burst of speed to catch up with Katie. She slipped her hand into the other girl's, giving it a reassuring squeeze, and Katie cast her a startled look.

"It's almost the eclipse," Katie whispered. Eleanor nodded.

The dark disk of the moon was steadily gliding in front of the sun, like a lid sliding over a pot. The air grew dimmer. It was already as dark as late afternoon, tilting into evening. That cobweb feeling was getting more intense.

Eleanor tried angling toward the side of the path, but she couldn't turn, even a tiny bit. Katie checked her watch. "A minute and a half to totality," she said. "We're going to flunk our project."

Eleanor let out a strangled laugh. "I really don't think we should worry about that right now," she said. Then she spotted something up ahead.

It was hard to make out in the darkening gloom, but Eleanor could just see the pale ribbons of two more paths, all three meeting in a three-way crossroads. And there were figures on the other paths, too—two people on each.

"Oh no," she said.

Pip got there first, striding up as soon as she spotted the others, her companion trailing well behind. Then Eleanor and Katie arrived, and Otto and his friend, who looked just as frightened as Katie.

Actually, she looked a lot like Katie, if Katie was two inches taller and a bit skinnier and wore makeup and slinky black tops.

"Otto," Pip said quietly. Gloaming was in her hand, bare steel glinting softly even in the near-total darkness. "Who is your friend?"

"This is Katie?" he said. "And that's—" He looked at Eleanor.

"Katie," she said, edging away from the girl with tear-streaked cheeks who was suddenly looking a lot less terrified.

"And this is Katie, too," Pip said casually, stepping forward and turning at the same time to put herself between Eleanor and Otto.

Pip's lab partner was the tallest of the three Katies. Her hair was back in a single, severe braid, and she looked older than the others, more serious. Her head tilted as she examined the three friends, and the other two Katies copied the movement perfectly.

"This worked far better than I'd hoped," they said in unison, their voices so closely matched it was almost hard to tell there was more than one. The shorter Katies stepped closer to the one in the center, and the air sort of *flexed*, and then there was only one Katie—a tall woman with colorless white hair that flowed in ringlets down to her waist. She wore a gray dress. At her throat was a black ribbon from which hung a silver pendant: a full moon flanked by two crescents facing in opposite directions.

Pip lifted Gloaming, standing in front of the other two protectively.

"You're Mr. January's other sister," Eleanor said.

"Of course," Katie replied. "In your world, I go by the name Katie Rhodes. Though sometimes I have been compared to—"

"Hekate," Pip said. She was an expert in mythology, especially since Halloween. "Goddess of witchcraft and crossroads. Right?"

"But the clock isn't ticking," Otto said.

"Isn't it?" Katie said, and made a twisting gesture with her hand.

All at once, the color bled out of the world. The ticking of the clock became like thunder, and the hairs on the back of Eleanor's neck stood on end.

"The error my siblings made was in giving you warning. I ensured you had none. You are in my crossroads, and when the totality of the eclipse is over, you will be mine for good." She wasn't smiling or gloating, the way her siblings would have. She sounded matter-of-fact.

Eleanor wheeled toward the edge of the path. If they could escape the crossroads, maybe that would be enough to get free of Katie's grasp.

"I wouldn't," Katie said mildly as Eleanor sprinted for the woods.

She'd barely gotten a toe over the edge when something slammed into her, throwing her back to the ground. Otto yelped and hurried to help her back to her feet. Pip launched herself toward another spot at the edge of the road—and then she was being lifted off her feet and tossed back by some unseen force. At least Pip landed nimbly on her feet, scowling. Eleanor stared at the empty air—and suddenly it wasn't so empty. For a split second, the air shimmered with a strange light.

But she didn't just see it. She felt it. She felt the *roads*, the only real thing in this place. She could sense them stretching out, away from the crossroads. They seemed to call to her. They seemed to be waiting for her to answer.

"We have to try to get away from the crossroads," Otto suggested under his breath.

"You cannot run faster than my hounds," Katie said. She whistled an eerie two-tone note. Rag-a-bone and Shatterblack slinked out from behind her, as if they had been hidden in her silhouette. They paced a wide circle around the trio, moving in opposite directions until each of them blocked the way down one of the roads, Katie herself barring the third path.

Eleanor looked around wildly in the gloom—and then her eyes fixed on the horizon. At first she thought there was something huge and solid hurtling toward them, and then she realized what she was seeing was pure darkness. The darkness of the total eclipse, moving like a wave over the woods.

Instinctive terror swept through her. She gave a cry and reached for her friends. They caught her hands just as the moon slid over the last sliver of the sun.

Only the candlewick eyes of the umbral hounds broke through the solid dark that fell across them then. Eleanor shivered. The night was so thick she could feel it against her skin.

It felt so strange. *She* felt strange.

Eleanor's breath came raggedly. The Story—the worldwalker. Is that what she felt, seeping into her skin, making the dark feel alive?

No. She wouldn't let the Story take her. She couldn't.

Katie snapped her fingers. A light appeared, floating in the air beside her. Its light was pale and colorless. Everything was colorless—their eyes and hair and skin and clothes, and the road itself. All the color had bled out of the world.

"It won't be long," Katie said, almost wearily. "Two minutes, and totality will be over. You can stop running. You will become the keys to open our way home, and we will return."

She didn't sound triumphant or mocking, the way Mr. January and Mrs. Prosper had been when they thought themselves on the verge of victory. Instead, her voice held a note of—was it dread? Reluctance?

"You don't have to do this," Eleanor said.

Katie's eyes were tiny pinpricks of light like stars. "It's everything we've been working toward for centuries. We will open the gates of the Pallid Kingdom and our parents' armies will spill out. This world and all the rest will be drowned in gray, and we will wear our crowns of silver and bone. And I will be the one that made it happen. I will be rewarded."

Her words were sharp with hunger and longing and fear, and she stalked toward them in the darkness. Shatterblack and Rag-a-bone came, too, and Eleanor and the others drew together. Pip dropped Eleanor's hand to bring Gloaming up, facing Rag-a-bone in a defensive pose.

Katie stretched out a hand. One fingertip touched Eleanor's cheek. Her skin was cold. "It won't hurt," she said, like it mattered at all.

They were out of time, and there was no one to help them. Nothing that could save them.

Unless . . .

We need more time, Eleanor thought desperately. They had to get away from this place. And there was only one way she could think of to do it. She shut her eyes. *You want me, Story? Come on. Open a road with me. Let's walk between the worlds.*

The Story answered. Something cold and poisonous and lovely flowed through her veins. Taking hold. She gasped, her eyes flying open. Strange threads of light gleamed around her like a spiderweb, and the filaments stretched out in all directions.

They were all connected. All the worlds. And she could feel them. Here at the crossroads of the Wending, she could feel every one, all at once, and all she had to do was *reach out*—

"The sun!" Pip cried in horror. The faintest sliver of light shone at the edge of the moon. Totality was ending.

Eleanor's heart thudded in her chest. She could do this. She could be the world-walker and she could find a way to get out of this place.

Help us, she thought.

"No!" Katie cried, but it was too late.

Power twined around Eleanor. The world-walker's power. *Her* power. She reached out blindly, grabbing at whatever threads she could.

Take us away. Anywhere but here. We need more time, more time, more time, she thought desperately, her words skipping along with her frantic heartbeat.

A road appeared, knitting itself out of nothing beside them. A fourth road, unguarded.

"Run!" Eleanor cried. Otto didn't hesitate—he dashed for the road, and Pip plunged after him. Eleanor sprinted to follow.

The startled hounds hesitated half a second—and no more. Shatterblack leaped. Eleanor half-turned, flinging out a hand to protect herself from the hound's leap.

The thread of moonlight around her wrist unknotted itself at her gesture. It arced gracefully through the air and lashed at Shatterblack's muzzle. The hound shrieked and leaped back, and her sister barked in alarm.

"Where are we going?" Otto called.

The road didn't lead anywhere. Not yet. Eleanor could sense it the same way she could feel her own hand at the end of her arm. And she could sense the Wending, too. Waiting. But she didn't know how to tell it where they needed to go. Her mind was a jumble.

We need more time. We need to get away. She's after us. Katie Rhodes. The People Who Look Away. We need—I need—I want—

All her fear and desire seemed to well up inside of her, swirling together into a storm—

She stretched out her hand.

The forest seemed to tear in two, a new landscape bleeding into the space where it had been. Different trees, a thicket of pale birches. "Go!" Eleanor yelled as the others gaped.

Two steps, three, and they were on the new road. She could *feel* the way the roads knit together, the way they might come apart. Rag-a-bone and Shatterblack streaked toward them, and on instinct Eleanor raised her hand, and *willed* the roads apart.

Where the two roads met, the air shimmered, wobbled. Where the edges of the two roads met, they frayed and shrank back. Only a thin seam of dirt and grass divided them, but the hounds rebounded as if they'd struck a wall.

And then Katie and the hounds and the gnarled forest and the eclipse-darkened sky were gone. They stood in the pale light of morning in a forest of white birch trees, a dirt path beneath their feet.

And they weren't alone.

"What have you done?" a hard voice asked. Eleanor turned, the world still spinning around her and the world-walker's power like electricity in her blood. For a moment she stared, not understanding what she was seeing. *Who* she was seeing.

The woman standing a few feet away crossed her arms, looking angry.

"Mom?" Eleanor managed.

And then her legs went out from under her.

Seven

Eleanor dreamed of twisting roads and the glitter of sharp glass stars, and woke to arguing voices. One of the voices rose, angry and sharp. "What do you expect to do about it? You're hardly more than a girl; there's so little of the warrior in you."

Eleanor knew that voice. Her eyes snapped open and she bolted upright. She had been lying with Otto's hoodie bundled under her head, among the roots of a tree on a bed of strangely colorless moss. Now she struggled up to her feet. A few yards away, looking haggard and cross, stood Pip, Otto—and Eleanor's mother.

Eleanor's knees wobbled again, but she forced herself to stay upright and swallowed down a wordless cry. Her mother looked exactly as she had the last time Eleanor had seen her. Harder and sharper than her mother ought to be, her eyes slate gray and her mouth set in a firm, unbent line.

The woman's expression flickered faintly with interest, but not with warmth or recognition or love. This was not Claire Barton. It was the hedgewitch. The Story was the only thing left, but still Eleanor wanted to run to her and wrap her arms around her.

More than that, she wanted the woman to run to *her,* arms outstretched.

But Eleanor's mother was gone. *Gone, gone, gone,* said the beating of her heart, and her whole body ached with the word.

Eleanor curled her fingers under, letting her fingernails dig into her palms. She drew in a long breath through her nose. And she made her heart as cool and clear as glass.

Pip gave a wordless cry and strode across the mossy forest floor, pulling Eleanor into a tight hug. Eleanor shut her eyes to block out the sight of the woman who wasn't her mother and buried her face in Pip's shoulder. Otto hung back, but he lifted up his fingertips in not-quite-a-wave, and she mirrored the gesture.

"You're awake," Pip said, and her voice was ragged with relief. "You had us seriously freaked out."

"How long was I out?"

"Only a few minutes," Pip assured her.

That was a relief, at least. "Where are we?" Eleanor asked. She looked around, mostly so that she didn't have to look at the stranger who looked like her mother. They stood in a drab forest. The trees were spindly, their leaves withered on their branches. A cold gray light filtered down, the sky overcast and dull.

"This is another world, isn't it?" Eleanor asked wonderingly. "I brought us here."

The hedgewitch grunted disdainfully. "The *Wending* brought us here. You merely told it where you wanted to go. And directed it to snatch me as well, it seems."

"I didn't mean to," Eleanor said, forcing herself to look at the hedgewitch.

"A strong desire doesn't always need to be spoken to be understood," the hedgewitch said. "Smart of you, though. I've done a fair amount of research on the Wending, after all."

Eleanor didn't say anything, but privately she thought that the hedgewitch didn't understand—if her desires and longings had brought the woman here, it wasn't because she was the hedgewitch, or a valuable ally, or anything like that. It was because Eleanor had been afraid.

And more than anything else, she'd wished her mother was there to comfort her.

Gone, gone, gone, said the beating of her heart, which wasn't cold glass after all, and Eleanor's throat constricted around a sob.

"Then I really am the world-walker now," Eleanor said dully.

The hedgewitch snorted. "You will be, in time. You certainly have not earned the right to call yourself that just yet," she said. She folded her arms, giving Eleanor a look that was deeply unimpressed. "Right now you are a foolish girl with a power she cannot begin to understand. A pity you won't live long enough to harness it."

Eleanor flinched. Even if this wasn't her mother, hearing the hedgewitch talk about their inevitable deaths left her feeling bruised and broken.

"You know, the *Thirteen Tales of the Gray* really didn't capture what a complete bummer the hedgewitch is," Pip said, rolling her eyes. The hedgewitch's lips pressed into a thin line, exactly the expression Eleanor's mother made when she was annoyed, and Eleanor looked quickly away.

"Much as I would *love* to stick around, I am in the middle of a research project," the hedgewitch said. "So if you could ask the Wending to open a road for me, I'd be much obliged."

Eleanor gritted her teeth, anger flaring at the hedgewitch—for being rude, for being unhelpful, for being the wrong person entirely. Even these few minutes with the woman made her feel ill. Her mother was dead, and this *thing* looked like her, and it was so strange she couldn't even feel grief—just this horrible, stomach-churning wrongness.

"Fine," Eleanor snapped. "I didn't mean to bring you here anyway."

She turned away, unable to stand looking at the hedgewitch. She stared down the dirt road, trying to see all the shimmering threads she'd used before. Find the threads—grab hold of them—open a road.

She stared. And waited. She willed the bright threads to appear, for a new road to spin itself out of nothing, for another world to unfold before her.

But nothing happened.

Eight

Eleanor had been trying for half an hour to open the Wending again. All she'd gotten out of it was a headache.

"I think I wore out the world-walker's world-walking," she said, slumping in defeat.

The hedgewitch let out a noise of frustration. "Ripping your way through the Wending—what were you thinking?"

"I was thinking we were going to die," Eleanor snapped.

The hedgewitch huffed. "Well, you didn't. And now we're all stuck here until you recover."

"Where *is* here?" Otto asked, looking around at the anemic woods. "I mean, a forest, obviously. But what world?"

The hedgewitch gave a long-suffering sigh. "I'll go and see if I can find out," she said. "Don't go anywhere without me." She turned on her heel, stalking down the road.

Pip squinted after her. "Your mom's kind of terrible."

"Says the girl whose mom tried to *ritually sacrifice us,*" Otto pointed out.

Pip shrugged. "I said terrible, not evil. There's a difference."

Eleanor sank down onto the squiggly end of a root and stared out at the forest. Pip sat next to her. She wrapped her arms around Eleanor, resting her chin on Eleanor's shoulder. Otto sat on the other side, leaving a bit of distance between them, but that was a sign of how much he cared about her, too. She'd started to feel overwhelmed when both of them hugged her at the same time, like she was getting claustrophobic. So now they took turns.

Eleanor stared straight ahead, eyes focused on nothing. A stranger was in her mother's place. And the same thing was going to happen to Pip. To all of them. It was all too much. If she thought about it for even a moment, she was afraid she might break apart.

"We'll find a way to get her back, you know," Pip said. "We'll stop Mr. January. And the Stories. And we'll go home and everything will be great."

"Since when are you an optimist?" Otto asked, lightly teasing.

Pip scrunched up her nose. "Ugh. It's Jack. The warrior, I mean. It's not even a little bit cynical. It's constantly convinced that we can save the day and live happily ever after."

"How dare it rob you of your doom and gloom?" Otto asked, and Pip chuckled.

"What about you?" Pip asked, squeezing Eleanor's shoulder. "Feel anything changing?"

"I don't know," Eleanor said. "I can't open the road, but if I really concentrate there's this sort of . . . shimmer." It was like a hum in the air—but also like her fingers were brushing against strings that were threaded between everything. There was one running between Pip and Otto. She wasn't sure what it was, except that it was strong and bright and *loud*. But when she tried to reach out, like she had when she opened the road . . . nothing.

She sighed.

"You probably just need to rest," Otto reassured her.

"It feels like trying to work a strained muscle," Eleanor said. She rolled her shoulders.

A strange sound came from the direction where the hedgewitch had vanished. A metallic scrape, and then a cut-off yell. Eleanor was on her feet before she fully processed what she'd heard.

"What was that?" Otto asked.

"Nothing good," Pip said, rising as well. Her hand on Gloaming, she advanced down the road. Eleanor and Otto stuck close as they followed. The road wound around the side of a small hill, blocking their view up ahead. They rounded the corner slowly—and froze.

The hedgewitch was on her knees, hands held up in surrender. Around her stood four figures clad in dark gray armor that was pinched and twisted in strange, thorny shapes. Each of them carried a long, jagged spear—and the tip of one was pointed right between the hedgewitch's shoulder blades.

One of the armored figures turned its head toward the trio. His lips parted, and he inhaled deeply through his nose—as if smelling them. The hedgewitch, her hair wild around her face, looked at them with wide, frightened eyes.

"Run!" she called, her voice harsh as the caw of a crow. Otto seized Eleanor's arm, turning to flee—but Eleanor stood rooted to the spot.

She couldn't leave her mother there. She couldn't abandon her.

"Run, you fools!" the hedgewitch shouted, but it was too late. Two of the gray-armored soldiers closed the distance in a few long strides. The jagged tip of a spear hovered an inch from Eleanor's throat, and cold, empty eyes stared into hers. The other spear was leveled at Pip, who grimaced and threw down Gloaming, raising her hands in surrender.

"I'm sorry," Eleanor said softly as a soldier's hand closed around her arm.

Their captors said nothing at all.

Nine

Their hands were bound behind their backs with thin rope that bit into their wrists, and the strange, silent soldiers marched them up the road. Otto tried to talk to them at first, but they only stared down at him, expressionless, and made pointed gestures with their spears.

Before long, they reached the edge of the trees. Here the dirt path met up with a sternly straight road of gray brick. It sliced its way cleanly through a rolling landscape of hills. At the end of the road, built within a blasted crater of rock and dirt, was their destination: a castle.

The massive structure loomed even from this distance. It was ringed by high, gray walls, and topped with looming gray towers. Above it streamed banners the color of soot.

"That doesn't look promising," Otto said. The soldier walking behind him shoved him hard on the shoulder.

The hedgewitch looked troubled. Her fingers worked behind her, twisting as if she were trying to get free of her bindings. At least Pip still had Gloaming. The third time they'd tried to take the sword from her, only to have it vanish and reappear at her hip, the soldiers had tied it down to its scabbard so that even if Pip got her hands free, she couldn't draw it. Eleanor didn't know what was waiting for them in the castle, but she was glad they had a weapon.

The gates opened as they approached. Fear gnawed relentlessly at Eleanor's insides, but she forced herself to keep moving, all too aware of the wicked weapons at her back.

Beyond the gates was a courtyard of stone as colorless as all the rest. To the left was a building that looked like a stable—but the creatures within it definitely weren't horses. Some had long bodies like greyhounds, with heads that split into writhing tendrils. Others were built like rhinoceroses, with the heads of wolves. They all stood deathly still in their stalls.

"What is this place?" Pip whispered, looking around with wide eyes. There were more men, women, and even children walking around, dressed in rough-spun clothes in shades of gray and brown, but all of them had the same blank expressions as the soldiers. None of them spoke. None of the animals made any noise. The only sound was the rasp of cloth and tramp of feet, and the metallic clanking of the soldiers' armor.

The silence made Eleanor's whole body shake with instinctive fear.

Come on. You're the world-walker. Do something, she screamed silently at herself—but concentrating as hard as she could, only the faintest shimmering lines traced through the air.

"What is this?" a voice said, and Eleanor almost cried out in surprise at the sudden breaking of the silence.

A boy who looked about sixteen approached from the right. His collarbones stood out from his skin, and his cheekbones jutted up above hollow cheeks. He wore a simple gray shirt, loose on his narrow frame but belted at the waist. Unlike everything else, he wasn't gray, but his brown hair had an ashen cast to it. A thin iron circlet sat on his head, like a crown.

One of the soldiers opened his mouth. Eleanor flinched back. It was a long, stretched O of black, no sign of anything inside but darkness—no tongue, no teeth, no throat. From that void came a sound like a cloud of flies, a soft and horrid buzzing.

The boy looked sharply at Eleanor and the others.

"In the woods? But you're not from the village," he said. His hands were folded behind his back as he stalked around them, looking them up and down. "Who are you?"

"Don't tell him anything," the hedgewitch hissed.

"You can tell me now, or you can tell my parents. And believe me, their questions are less kind than mine," the boy said. He stopped in front of Eleanor. His eyes met hers, and a shiver went through her. There was something about the boy that seemed familiar.

"Who are you?" the boy asked again, leaning closer. Eleanor clamped her teeth shut and glared at him.

"Let us go, and maybe we'll tell you," Pip suggested.

The boy straightened up. "Take them to the throne room."

They were herded toward the front doors of the castle. Eleanor looked over her shoulder, managing to catch Otto's gaze. He looked as panicked as she felt.

They were marched through a long hall, up a set of steps, and then through a massive pair of iron doors. Eleanor, pushed out in the front, found herself in a huge, vaulted room, the ceiling covered in intricate patterns of twisting lines. Columns lined each side of the vast hall, and a single red length of carpet split its center—the only color in the whole place.

Two spikes of onyx stone stood at the front, carved into thrones. And on those thrones sat two figures Eleanor had seen once before, in a painting on the wall of a hidden room in Mrs. Prosper's office. Fresh fear flooded Eleanor's body, followed by a slow wave of dread.

They were the Pallid King and the Pallid Queen. The mother and father of the People Who Look Away. Which could mean only one thing.

Somehow, impossibly, they were in the Pallid Kingdom.

"No, no, no," someone moaned, and Eleanor realized it was her. She stopped walking, but still the soldier dragged her forward, toward the grim thrones.

The king and queen were like people, but *stretched.* Their bodies and limbs long and horribly thin, even their faces distorted—not that they really *had* faces. They had no mouths, no noses, only black, lidless eyes. Their fingers, resting on the arms of their thrones, were like spiders' legs. They wore robes of many shades of gray, and above their heads floated a few jagged spurs of metal and stone, like shattered crowns.

Eleanor twisted to look back helplessly at the others. The hedgewitch's face was drained of blood, stark fear in her eyes. Pip and Otto looked terrified.

"*Why have you brought these vermin to our hall?*" someone whispered in Eleanor's ear. She gave a startled cry—but there was no one behind her. The Pallid Queen was leaning forward, and even though she was at least fifty feet away, Eleanor was somehow sure she had been the one to speak.

That fly-buzzing sound came from one of the soldiers again, and the queen clicked her stretched-out fingers against the arm of her throne. "*Then our child can explain himself.*"

A door to the side of the hall opened. The boy from before came in, shoulders back and head up, stiff as a soldier. Behind him walked two younger children, both girls. The older one was about Eleanor's age, with plain brown hair hanging in a single long braid down her back, strange purple flowers woven into it. The younger girl had red-gold hair, braided the same way, and her eyes were a bright, startling green.

A shiver went down Eleanor's spine. Because she'd seen these children before, too. Just not their faces—because those had been turned away, in the painting in Mrs. Prosper's office.

They couldn't be the same children, Eleanor thought. The children in the painting were the People Who Look Away. And the People Who Look Away were adults. Unless . . .

The Wending could take you to any world. Worlds that *are* and worlds that *were* and worlds that could have been. Did that mean it could take them into the past?

They'd been wondering where they were. They should have been wondering *when.*

"*Why did you have these four brought before us?*" the Pallid King whispered, and just as the queen's voice had, his voice seemed to come from just over Eleanor's shoulder. Like he was leaning down behind her. She steeled herself and tried to keep from shaking.

"They were in the woods. They aren't from the village. Their clothes are strange," the boy—the prince?—said, stepping forward. "I thought you would want to see them."

"*Bring one of them to us,*" the queen whispered.

The boy nodded. He walked toward them and paused, eyes roving over the four of them. The hedgewitch straightened, opened her mouth as if to volunteer—but then the boy stepped forward and grabbed Eleanor's elbow, pulling her toward the steps of the dais on which the two thrones sat.

"Hey! Leave her alone!" Pip called, and then grunted like something had hit her in the stomach. Eleanor twisted in time to see her on her knees, wheezing, and Otto being restrained by another one of the soldiers. Eleanor held back a whimper and turned back to the front. She couldn't bear to lift her eyes to the faces of the king and queen.

The queen leaned forward. Her eyes were round and lidless, and Eleanor could see herself reflected in each one. She looked small and terrified.

She *was* terrified. Her mouth was dry, and she shook so hard she didn't know if she could stay standing if the boy took his hand from her arm.

"*Who are you?*" the queen asked in that horrible whisper. Eleanor didn't think she could speak if she wanted to. She swallowed and stayed silent. The queen laughed softly, a dry and scuttling sound. "*You think that you are being brave. You think that what you do here matters, but it does not. There is no purpose to your silence. Where did you come from, child? The mountains? Across the sea? Beneath some rock we neglected to turn over?*"

Eleanor clamped her back teeth together and didn't say a word.

The queen sat up once more. She considered Eleanor, tapping a single finger in a slow, relentless rhythm. "*Melia. Come.*"

The older girl flinched, then stepped forward. She moved like a deer picking its way out into the open as she approached the dais. She was beautiful, Eleanor thought—an aching, perfect kind of beautiful that made Eleanor feel tense. As if a single flaw, a hair out of place or a smudge of dirt, would be disaster.

Behind her, the younger girl shivered—and split apart. A second, identical girl darted away, hiding quickly behind a column. Eleanor blinked. She didn't think the king or queen had noticed. The little girl must be Katie, with her ability to split into multiple versions of herself, which meant the other girl was Mrs. Prosper—but her first name had been Korri, not Melia.

Katie, Mrs. Prosper, Mr. January—those were the names they'd chosen for Eleanor's world. Of course they weren't their original names, Eleanor realized.

"Dearest Mother. Honored Father. What do you wish of me?" Melia asked. Her voice was smooth as polished stone, but her fingers knotted behind her back.

"*What would you use to make this girl speak the truth?*" the whisper asked.

Melia tipped her chin up, answering confidently. "A tincture of angelica and yew would encourage honest answers."

"That is correct. Yet it would not force her to speak. She could remain silent. Ash."

The boy holding Eleanor's arm stiffened. "Yes, Mother?" he asked.

"How would you make this girl speak?"

Ash looked down at Eleanor. She stared up at him. Could this really be Mr. January? He looked so young. And there was something in his eyes she'd never seen in Mr. January's.

Sympathy.

"Pain might make her speak," Ash said. "But she would give up more readily to save one of her companions. A bargain, perhaps. Spare them suffering in return for her answers."

He sounded so matter-of-fact. It made Eleanor's skin crawl.

"An interesting approach. Thea."

Then came the younger girl, scurrying forward to take her place at her sister's side. Eleanor noted the tiny twitch in Ash's fingers against her arm, and the way Melia tensed, trying not to look over at her sister. The younger girl bounced up nervously on the balls of her feet before curtsying and settling.

"Which of this girl's companions would she break her silence to save?"

Thea glanced between her siblings, her expression one of plain terror. They stared straight ahead. Eleanor's mouth was dry. She could feel their nervousness.

She's Katie Rhodes. She's evil, Eleanor reminded herself, but it was hard to remember as the little girl trembled.

"I—I'm not sure," Thea stammered. There was a moment of silence that seemed louder than a shout. And then the king crooked one finger, beckoning Thea closer. She hesitated, then crept forward. "But I don't—I don't know—" she started.

"*Enough babbling.*" The king's whisper admonished Thea. She fell quiet as she scaled the steps to the dais on which the thrones sat. The Pallid King reached out his spidery hand, his crooked fingers caressing her golden hair. "*If you wish to make her speak, you choose the smallest. The weakest. The one least able to stand the pain.*"

Those slender fingers wrapped around Thea's neck and shoulder, resting loosely but holding her in place. Ash's hand tightened on Eleanor's arm, his breath coming faster. He was afraid, too, Eleanor thought. Afraid for himself? Or for Katie—Thea?

Was it possible, Eleanor wondered, that the People Who Look Away could care about someone?

"Ash. My son, my eldest. You have taken something that belongs to us. Where is it?"

"I don't know what you mean," Ash said immediately.

"Melia. Your brother's mouth is filled with lies. You will aid him in honesty."

Melia shuddered. She twisted her hands in the air in front of her, and a glass vial appeared in her hands, filled with an amber-colored liquid. She turned, holding it out to Ash. Eleanor thought she saw her mouth *I'm sorry.*

"*Drink,*" the whisper ordered. Ash hesitated. Then he let go of Eleanor's arm and stepped toward his sister. He took the vial, and tipped it up, draining the whole thing. He dropped the vial to the ground. The glass shattered, but no one moved.

Eleanor, forgotten, fell back a step. She looked around wildly. Pip was on the floor on her stomach, with a soldier's boot on her back holding her down as she bared her teeth. Otto sat with his legs flung out in front of him, like he'd gotten knocked down, too. Only the hedgewitch was still standing, unmoving.

"*Where is that which you have stolen from us?*" the king asked.

Ash stared down at the ground and said nothing. The queen hissed in displeasure. Eleanor fell back another step, but none of the soldiers or royals seemed to be paying attention to her anymore. She edged to the side, toward the columns, and looked back again at her friends.

The air shifted. Shimmers of light played around her. Those bright threads running all around her sprang into focus, and she could *feel* them—still faintly, but there.

"*Thea, my darling, come here. Let us find out if we can make your brother break his silence,*" the queen whispered.

Thea let out a whimper, and Eleanor went cold. What were they going to do?

"Eleanor." The hedgewitch locked eyes with Eleanor. "Use your power. Get out of here."

The queen had wrapped one horribly long hand around Thea's shoulder. All eyes were fixed on the two of them. Eleanor looked wildly at the hedgewitch. At Pip and Otto. She couldn't run. She couldn't leave her friends.

"You can't help us if you're trapped with us. Go," the hedgewitch hissed. The soldier beside her shoved her hard, and she fell to one knee. Then he began to turn toward Eleanor.

Just as Thea started to scream.

Eleanor turned away from her friends and bolted for the edge of the room.

The soldiers weren't fast in their armor, and she had a second's head start. It was enough to sprint around behind one of the columns, to screw her eyes shut, to reach for the worldwalker's power blindly and *pull*—

She was still weak. But a tiny shimmer in the air turned into a whisker-thin seam of light, and then eased wider—a tiny gap in the fabric of the world, wide enough to slip through. She didn't care what was on the other side. She turned herself to the side and toppled through.

She landed on the other side awkwardly, her bound hands crushed under her body, already willing the tear in the world shut. The portal vanished.

Eleanor lay on the cold stone floor, breathing heavily. That hadn't been the Wending—there hadn't been a road. And with as little strength as she had, she didn't think she'd gotten far.

She pushed herself to her feet, looking around. She was in a familiar stone corridor. She hadn't even gotten outside the castle walls. She groaned. What good was getting away from the throne room if she was still trapped in here, her hands tied?

And her friends left behind. Guilt roiled inside her. If she'd run in the first place, when she saw the hedgewitch with the soldiers, maybe Pip and Otto would still be free. But now she'd gotten them all captured—and then abandoned them. With no plan or hope of rescuing them.

A hand touched Eleanor's elbow. She managed not to shout as she twisted around.

The younger girl was standing behind her, eyes wide. Her hair was in loose waves, falling around her shoulders, instead of its orderly braid, and her clothing was different than it had been in the throne room. Eleanor remembered the other little girl, darting away.

"How did you get out here?" the girl asked curiously. *Katie,* Eleanor thought. *Or Thea. Or whoever she is.* Eleanor clamped her lips together. The girl frowned. "You can't stay here. The Empty will find you. I'll show you a place to hide." She beckoned.

"Why should I trust you?" Eleanor demanded. "You're probably going to lead me right back to those soldiers."

The girl shrugged miserably. "I guess you shouldn't. But if you stay here, they'll definitely get you. Please?" She backed away down the hall, clearly inviting Eleanor to follow.

Eleanor looked the other way. Cold stone and no sign of safety. She bit her lip. If she was right, if this girl Thea was really Katie Rhodes, surely Eleanor shouldn't trust her.

But maybe she wasn't evil *yet*. And it wasn't like Eleanor had much of a choice.

"Fine," Eleanor said. Thea smiled and scurried away. Eleanor hustled to follow, moving awkwardly with her hands tied behind her back. Thea skittered around turns, dodging out of the path of more silent servants as they went. Finally they came to what seemed to be a dead end—a flat expanse of wall. But Thea pressed her hand to a brick, and the wall slid to the side, opening a narrow passageway. Thea gave her one last smile, and slipped inside.

Eleanor stood, staring at the passage. Thea could be leading her into a trap. Given everything Eleanor knew about her, she almost certainly was.

Heavy footsteps sounded in the hallway around the corner. Eleanor took a deep breath, and dived in after Thea.

Ten

When Eleanor emerged she was standing in a small courtyard garden, wild with color.

It was so startling to see color at all that it took a moment for Eleanor to realize that the colors here were all *wrong*. Blue leaves trembled on bushes festooned with green flowers. The grass was rust brown, the tree trunks a deep purple.

Eleanor stared, her thoughts a tangle.

She'd just run away. She'd left her friends there. Guilt and fear and anger were like cracks spreading over her heart. She felt like she was going to break apart.

"Miss?" Thea said. Eleanor wrenched her gaze to the girl, her heart still pounding.

"What's going to happen to my friends?" she croaked.

"They'll be taken to the dungeons," Thea said. "But you won't be able to get to them. They'll be Emptied like all the others. You can't stop it."

"Emptied? What does that mean?" she demanded.

"Everything they used to be is wiped away. The only thing left is obedience. The soldiers out there, they're Empty, too," Thea said. Eleanor had a vision of Pip in gray armor, face as blank as the soldiers, a jagged spear in her hands.

"Don't worry. They don't come here," Thea said, but that wasn't what Eleanor was worried about at all. Thea seemed to realize this, and bit her lip. "Here. Let me untie you."

Her small fingers made quick work of the knots. Eleanor massaged her wrists, which were crisscrossed with angry red marks.

Thea gave a sudden shudder. She wrapped her arms around herself and sank down into a crouch. "Sorry," she whispered. "They'll be finished soon."

"Finished?" Eleanor echoed. She dropped her voice. "Your parents. You're still in the throne room, aren't you?"

Thea nodded. "Some of me. As little as I could manage without them noticing. It's all right. I can stand it, as long as I concentrate on being *here* instead of in there. It's easier if I stay distracted." She bit her lip. "Usually, Ash—he tells me stories," she said.

"Ash. Your brother," Eleanor said. Mr. January telling his little sister stories was not an image she had ever considered. "I could tell you a story," Eleanor said softly.

"Please," Thea whispered.

They walked to a garden bench, the only thing in the garden

that seemed like a reasonable color, and sat together. Eleanor's mind spun with worry for her friends. But she couldn't help them right this second. She could help Thea.

"Once upon a time," she began.

She found herself telling Thea one of the stories from *Thirteen Tales of the Gray—The Girl Who Danced with the Moon.*

"Where did you learn that story?" Thea asked dreamily when Eleanor was done, her eyes distant and her hand trembling where it rested on her thigh.

"It's from a book," Eleanor said.

"You have books? We're not allowed to have books," Thea said. She got a wistful look on her face. "Once I heard about a place that has every story from every world. A clever thief steals *his* story and changes it to make himself rich."

Every story from every world. Where had Eleanor heard that before? "The Library of Endersea," she said. Wander had told her about that, hadn't she?

"That's it. The Library of Endersea," Thea repeated. She sighed. "I'd like to go there."

At that moment, there was a soft *shush* of cloth against stone, and Ash himself emerged into the garden, followed closely by Melia and by Thea, who looked wretched. Her skin was pale, tinged with gray, her hair limp and dull.

Eleanor's Thea stood and walked over to her, and the air flexed as it had on the path back home. Suddenly there was only one girl, looking exhausted.

Ash stared at Eleanor. "They're searching the castle for you," he said.

"And are you going to tell them where I am?" Eleanor asked, a challenge in her voice.

"You can't tell," Thea said, grabbing his hand. "They'll Empty her. You know they will."

"We should take her back right now. Maybe we won't get in trouble. Let Mother and Father deal with her," Melia said.

Ash was watching Eleanor with narrowed eyes. She glared back at him. Thea might just be a little girl, but *this* was Mr. January. The one who'd caused every horrible thing she and her friends had gone through. The one who'd cursed Eden Eld in the first place. And he'd dragged her up in front of those horrible thrones, talking about hurting her friends. He was definitely already wicked.

A bush near Ash's foot rustled, and a small, gray form marched out, mewling furiously. Eleanor blinked in surprise. An extremely fluffy kitten planted itself at Ash's feet and set about attacking his bootlaces. And Ash broke into a grin—not sly like Mr. January's, but a genuinely delighted smile that lit up his whole face.

"There you are," he said with pleasure, and scooped up the kitten. It hissed and swatted at him, flailing in his grip. "Don't worry, we didn't give you up."

"I hope having a pet is worth putting Thea through all of that," Melia said icily.

"She never comes out for *me*," Thea complained.

Melia frowned. "That cat of Ash's is the reason you were punished, and you *like* it?"

Cat of Ash's. Mr. January had three animal servants. The huge and fearsome graveyard dog, the cruel rattlebird, and the sharp-witted, occasionally very helpful cat-of-ashes. The cat-of-ashes had helped them as much as she could—or as much as she felt like, at least. And this was *her.* A tiny, floofy, precious version of her. "Kitten-of-ashes," Eleanor whispered, and a half-hysterical giggle leaped to her lips. She clapped a hand over her mouth.

"She's so *cute,*" Eleanor laughed, and gasped. The kitten hissed fiercely at her and swiped a paw through the air. Tiny sparks rained from her claws.

"I rescued her from the Empty," Ash said, looking mildly concerned as Eleanor wheezed with laughter, her eyes watering.

The kitten-of-ashes. Her grown-up self would *kill* Eleanor for seeing this. The thought sent Eleanor into a fresh spate of giggles, but she bit the inside of her cheek hard to stop them.

She knew the laughter wasn't really because it was funny. She knew it was because she was too scared and worried and frantic to go on. But that didn't make it any easier to keep the laughter from erupting every time the kitten bared her little white fangs.

Ash cradled the kitten against his chest and stroked her ears. She still looked grumpy, but a raspy purr started up in her throat. Eleanor stared. The cat-of-ashes *hated* Mr. January. And here she was, two pounds of fluff and spite, cuddling up to him.

This was all so weird. Eleanor collapsed onto the garden bench, elbows on her knees, the effort of keeping her laughter inside making her chest ache. Ash handed the kitten-of-ashes off to Thea and approached, hands folded formally behind his back.

"You. Stop laughing," he ordered. In that instant he sounded quite a bit like Mr. January.

This, at last, was enough to shut Eleanor up.

"You and your friends. You wear strange clothes. You speak strangely. You don't *feel* right," he said, his gaze boring into her. "And you escaped the throne room without anyone seeing you."

"And?" Eleanor asked.

"You're from another world, aren't you?" he asked. Eleanor stilled, trying not to give anything away, but he made a soft sound of satisfaction. "I knew it. How did you get here?"

"Why should I tell you anything?" she asked.

He considered. "Let's make a deal," he said. If she'd shut her eyes, heard only his voice, she'd know for sure who he was in that moment.

"I know better than to make a deal with you," she said.

He looked puzzled. "Don't you want to hear what it is before you refuse it?" he asked.

She gritted her teeth. She didn't want to make any kind of bargain with Mr. January—even this younger, possibly less horrible version who liked cats. But she said, "Fine. What deal?"

"I'll help you and your friends escape. Thea and Melia will help, too," he said.

"In exchange for what?"

He smiled. It was not a smile as cruel as Mr. January's smile, but she could see the sharp points at its corners. "Simple. We help you escape. You leave this world the way you came. And you take us with you."

Eleven

Eleanor stared up at Ash. "You can't leave on your own?" she asked.

"Mother and Father have been searching for a way out of this world for ages, but they've never found one," Melia said. She was running her hands idly through Thea's hair. It had gone limp after her ordeal in the throne room, but now it sprang back thick and golden. Eleanor had the sense, though, that this was an illusion—nothing had truly changed.

"That means that if you take us with you, they won't be able to follow us," Ash said. "You have a way out, don't you? You got here, you must have a way to leave."

"Please," Thea said. Her eyes were wide and hopeful.

Eleanor wetted her lips, looking quickly between the siblings. What if she helped them get away, and that was the reason the curse existed in the first place? But what if she helped them get away, and it changed the future so that the curse never happened?

She wished Otto were here. He would rattle off a half-dozen theories about time travel and paradoxes and changing the timeline, and at the end of it she'd still have no idea what was going on, but she'd know they could figure it out.

"What will you do? If you escape, I mean," Eleanor said.

"Does it matter?" Ash asked.

"Of course it matters. Are you going to—to build armies and conquer other worlds?" Eleanor asked.

Melia made a face. "That's what our parents want to do. Gather more prisoners to Empty and turn into soldiers and weapons and beasts so that we can conquer *more* worlds, get *more* prisoners." She walked over to the stone fountain in the middle of the garden. She peered down into the water and ran her fingers lightly over her face. Her features shifted—her nose getting smaller, her jaw stronger, her eyes larger. Her lips turned a deep red, and shimmering purple appeared on her eyelids. "There's nothing beautiful here. I hate it," she said distantly.

"There are so many worlds, and I've never gotten to see any of them," Thea said. "I want to see *all* of them. Go *everywhere*."

Ash chuckled fondly. "I don't know if you'll have time to see *all* of them," he said.

Thea shrugged. "Then the sooner I get started, the better," she said, and he grinned. He loved her. There was no other explanation for the way he was looking at his sister. He adored her, and Eleanor had never seen Mr. January show the slightest bit of affection for *anything*.

"What about you?" she asked him.

He lifted a shoulder. "I don't know. I haven't thought that far. I just want to get me and my sisters out of here."

Eleanor looked between them, troubled. It was strange. They were nothing like the People Who Look Away—not yet. But it was like she could see exactly how they would get there, in this horrible place. How it would turn them wicked.

How Ash would learn more and more to bargain and lie. How Melia would put on false faces until there wasn't a real one left. And Thea—little Thea, splitting herself into pieces.

How could you stay whole in a place like this?

She didn't want to feel *sorry* for the People Who Look Away. And she wasn't sure she should. Whatever may have happened to them, they'd still done horrible things.

But with a shock she realized that maybe, just maybe, they might have ended up different. Maybe they still could.

"Do you think it's possible to change what happens to us?" Eleanor said softly.

"You mean like fate?" Ash asked.

"Fate. Yeah, I guess," she said. "Do you think that people are stuck with who they're meant to be, and there's no way to change it?"

"People can change," Melia said, still brushing her fingertips across the surface of the water. "We do it to people all the time."

Eleanor looked at her in confusion. Melia's expression was placid.

"Our parents don't just make the Empty. We have all kinds of ways to turn people into useful things. But they have to have the right ingredients for what you need. Say you want to make a sword. You can't make a weapon out of a gentle child. So either you find a violent man, or you change the child."

"They turn people into swords?" Eleanor asked, aghast.

Melia shrugged. "Or monsters, or mirrors, or statues, or—"

"Keys?" Eleanor suggested, a chill running down her spine.

"Sure. Twins are good for that. You make one a lock and one a key. The lock is impossible to pick, or open with a copied key, because it always knows its twin."

"Just about everything in this castle is made from bits of people's personalities and emotions," Ash said. "But these days all the villagers have inside them is dread and hopelessness. You can make good stones out of dread, and hopelessness makes good chains, but they're not good for much else. That's why they want to find a way to reach other worlds."

"Did you know you can Empty worlds, too?" Melia asked idly. "Suck out everything from them, until they collapse in on themselves, and everything inside dies. Or you can leave just the shell, all Empty and gray."

Eleanor thought of the gray world—the place where the People Who Look Away had taken all the cursed children of Eden Eld before them. Had they turned a whole living, thriving world into that terrible place? "That's horrible," she said with a shudder.

"Everything they do is horrible. That's why we want to leave," Ash said. "They're making us learn how to Empty people, too. Even Thea will have to learn soon."

Thea looked miserable. "They made me try once, and it's way worse than having it done to you. You have to be a different kind of empty, to do that to a person." A tear threatened at the corner of her eye, and she wiped it on her sleeve. Eleanor's heart squeezed.

Ash sat beside Eleanor on the bench. The kitten-of-ashes jumped down, trotting away to investigate a flower. "We want to change our fate. And you're the best chance we've found of doing it. Will you help us?"

Maybe this was how it all began. How the People Who Look Away got into Eleanor's world to do their wicked deeds.

Or maybe that was how they stopped Mr. January—not by defeating him, but by saving him. She had to believe that Ash was right. That they could change their fates. Because if the People Who Look Away could have a different future, Eleanor and her friends could, too.

"I'll help you escape," Eleanor said, her voice hoarse. "If we get my friends out of the dungeon, I can get all of us out of here."

Twelve

"Your friends are in the west cells in the dungeon. There are Empty guards on the doors. Only one way in or out. I don't see how we're going to manage it," Ash said. They were all sitting together on the ground under the tree in the garden, the kitten-of-ashes wandering around chasing specks of dust and leaving tiny scorch marks in the grass.

"Can you get in?" Eleanor asked.

"We're not permitted," Ash said. "And if they spot you, the Empty will send up an alarm."

She could open a portal into the dungeon—*maybe.* But even escaping the throne room had left her exhausted. What if she got them into the dungeon and couldn't get them back out?

Eleanor bit her lip, thinking. Usually she had Pip and Otto to bounce ideas around with and come up with a plan. Without them, her mind felt blank. Blank like the Empty.

Eleanor looked at Thea. Her bright, shiny hair tumbled around her shoulders—but Eleanor knew it was an illusion. "Melia, can you make us look like we're Empty with your illusions?" Eleanor asked.

Melia considered. "I could make us look right, but they'd still know. If we actually want to fool them, I have to Empty us. Not all the way. We'd recover. But it wouldn't be pleasant."

"If Thea can handle it, so can I," Eleanor said.

"That still leaves the problem of getting them all out," Ash said.

"If you can get us in, I can get us out," Eleanor said with more confidence than she felt.

"How?" Melia asked, leaning forward with bright interest in her eyes.

"I'll show you once we have my friends," Eleanor said.

"And you're certain it will work? We will only have one chance at this," Ash said.

"How long do we have before your parents decide to Empty one of my friends, or turn them into weapons?" Eleanor asked.

"Not long," Ash acknowledged.

She gave him a stubborn look. "Then I'm certain."

"We'll need time to prepare for the journey," Melia said, getting to her feet. "I'll Empty the three of you. I can't Empty myself. What is taken from you, you can get back. But what you take from yourself is gone forever. If I Empty myself, I'll be Empty forever."

"So I have to do it for her," Ash said. He swallowed, rubbing the back of his neck. "I'm not as good at it. If I get it wrong, I'll take the wrong things—things that won't grow back."

"You'll be fine," Melia told him, unbothered. "I need to get ready. Get my things. Ash, make sure she doesn't run off."

"Where would I go?" Eleanor asked, insulted, but Melia paid her no mind, striding off and vanishing through the gap in the wall. Eleanor blew out a huff of breath. Ash chuckled.

"She can be a bit slow to warm up to people," he said.

"Yeah?"

"I've been trying to get on her good side for fourteen years and it hasn't worked yet," he explained, and Eleanor laughed despite herself.

Thea's nose crinkled. "She's Mother's favorite. It's hard for her," she said. She'd pulled her knees up to her chest and was nervously plucking blades of violet grass.

Ash ruffled Thea's hair. "I know. You're right."

Thea looked intently at Eleanor. "Mother makes her stay for all of the Emptying. Makes her do it, too. She hates it so much, but she doesn't have a choice."

"That's why we're getting out of here," Ash told her reassuringly. The kitten-of-ashes sat by his foot and smacked the toe of his boot twice, insistently. He chuckled and scooped her up, turning her upside down in the crook of his arm. He tapped her nose affectionately. She sneezed sparks. "We're bringing you, too, little pest. Don't worry."

Eleanor shook her head wonderingly. Of all the strange and bewildering things she'd encountered, this was the hardest to understand.

She watched Ash and Thea play with the kitten-of-ashes, and tried not to think about the monsters she knew they would become.

MELIA RETURNED A short while later with the hedgewitch's bag slung over her shoulder. Eleanor leaped to her feet. "Where did you get that?" she asked.

"With the rest of the prisoners' things," Melia said. She had an excited gleam in her eye. "Who does it belong to?"

"My mother. Sort of," Eleanor said.

"Is the spell to cross between worlds in here?" Melia said curiously.

"I'll tell you how we're leaving once we have my friends back," Eleanor said. She didn't want them getting the idea that they didn't have to hold up their end of the bargain. In her time, the siblings were pretty strict about keeping their promises, but she didn't know if it was the same now.

"Let's get started, then," Melia said. She beckoned them over, but Eleanor hung back. Now that it was time, the thought of being Emptied was suddenly terrifying.

"You're sure it won't be permanent?" Eleanor asked, flinching away.

Melia looked impatient. "I already told you. The only way to make it permanent is to Empty you all the way or if you Empty yourself."

"Right. Okay," Eleanor said. She drew forward. She'd agreed to go first, but now she was regretting it. What if this was a trap? What if they were only pretending to want to escape? What if—

Melia's fingertips brushed against Eleanor's temples. Melia looked deep into her eyes. For a moment Eleanor felt only her cool touch, and then there was a sharp pinch that shot down to the very center of her body.

It felt like she was a pumpkin getting its guts scooped out. It didn't *hurt*, exactly, but it might have been better if it did.

Melia was kind, at least. She took Eleanor's fear first, so there was only one quick blaze of panic and then she could stand calmly as other parts of her were sheared away. She hadn't understood what it would mean to be Empty until she felt it happening. Grief—gone. The memory of her mother's face with the hedgewitch's eyes peering from it didn't inspire any sadness anymore. It was just a fact.

Friendship—that was torn away, too. Pip and Otto were people she knew, but she couldn't quite recall why she spent so much time with them.

The delight of her cousin Naomi's babble faded. The warm comfort of Jenny's arms wrapped around her went, too, and the simple wonder of looking up at the night sky. She wasn't truly Empty. Her memories remained, cluttering up her insides. But none of them had meaning anymore.

With every piece of her that vanished, the garden grew. Flowers bloomed; vines snaked up the walls. Was that where everything in the garden had come from? Pieces of people who had been Emptied?

"I have to leave you something," Melia had said. "Tucked away, but still there. Otherwise none of it will grow back."

When Melia stepped away, it took Eleanor a few dull seconds to find the fragment of herself that had been left. It took her another moment to realize what it was.

Determination.

They were going to get out of here.

"Eleanor?" Melia said. "Are you all right?"

"I'm fine," she said. Her voice was flat. All of her was flat.

Thea whimpered when Melia started to Empty her. Eleanor remembered that she would have felt bad for the girl a few minutes ago, but that was gone now. Soon enough, the garden was lusher than ever, and Thea walked over to Eleanor, standing placidly beside her.

"Now me," Melia said, and straightened her shoulders. Ash grimaced as he stretched out his hands, but Melia hardly blinked. It wasn't long before he stepped back, a frown on his face.

"Is something wrong?" Eleanor asked.

"No," he said. "It's just . . . that was easier than I expected."

"Because you are growing more skilled," Melia noted in a monotone. "May I begin?"

He nodded, and she reached for him.

When she was done they all stood, drab but not entirely colorless, and surveyed each other without emotion.

"I will need to apply the illusions to complete the effect," Melia said tonelessly.

Eleanor watched as Melia worked and found that she had a very different view of things. All her emotions and attachments had muddled things. They made it harder to see the truth and to make rational decisions.

It was a rational decision to rescue the others. She required Pip and Otto in order to defeat the curse, and the expertise of the hedgewitch was useful. But she was not as certain that cooperating with the siblings had been a logical choice. They would someday become her enemies. Why had she decided that she could trust them?

Because she felt sorry for them.

That is not a good reason to trust someone, she thought. And she'd ignored any misgivings she'd had after that because she was so worried about her friends. Another bad decision because of her feelings for other people.

Maybe she could get Melia to make being Empty permanent. Eleanor could stay this clearheaded forever.

"We should go," Eleanor said. Every moment of delay reduced their chances of escape.

"What about the kitten?" Thea asked. They looked down. The kitten-of-ashes was crouched against the grass, ears back.

"We agreed to take her," Ash said.

"If she doesn't behave, she might alert the Empty," Melia pointed out, and they all considered her point. "We were behaving irrationally. We shouldn't risk our lives for her."

"Agreed," Ash said.

"It's the smartest decision," Thea said, though that wasn't quite the same as agreeing.

Eleanor thought Melia was correct. They were taking a risk by bringing the kitten. It might get all of them captured. "No," she found herself saying, not quite sure why. "We agreed to take her. That makes it a promise. You shouldn't break promises." She bent and reached for the kitten, who swiped furiously at her. "I won't hurt you."

Reluctantly, ears pinned back, the kitten allowed herself to be picked up. Eleanor held her out toward Ash—he was the one who could hide her inside his shirt, since it was so loose. He looked at her a moment as if he was going to refuse, and then accepted the hissing little beast. He held her up at eye level.

"If you make noise, the Empty will find you and eat you," he informed her. The kitten fell silent, and when he tucked her inside his shirt she curled up in a little ball and didn't move.

They filed down the hall together. Up ahead, one of the Empty appeared. Eleanor didn't feel even the tiniest flutter of fear as the man strode past them. She could never have pretended to be this calm, she realized. She had so very much anxiety and fear and worry in her when she wasn't Empty, it was a wonder she got anything done. How easy. How simple it was, with nothing inside.

Around they went, and down, deep into the belly of the castle of the Pallid King and Queen. And then they came to the dungeons. The entrance was a thick iron door, narrow so that only one person could go through at a time. Ash took the lead, walking in a straight, steady line up to the door, where two Empty soldiers with jagged spears stood guard.

They filed in, one after the other. Eleanor followed the others into the dungeon, firmly deciding to request that Melia complete the process once they were out of here.

They went down another set of stairs, with colorless torches flickering in sconces beside them and water dripping somewhere, and then they reached a corridor lined with cells. The first several were empty, but halfway toward the back of the room a familiar figure sat slumped against the bars. Otto had his knees up to his chest and his gaze fixed blankly on the wall, and for a moment in the strange light, Eleanor thought he had been Emptied already

But then Otto looked toward them and bolted to his feet. He stared at her, and his mouth dropped open. "No," he breathed. "No, no—"

"It's an illusion," Eleanor said quickly, before he could panic and make too much noise.

Pip appeared at the bars of the opposite cell. Gloaming lay discarded on the ground by her feet, and the bars were covered with bright stripes where the metal had been gouged as if struck by the sword.

The hedgewitch peered out from the cell next to Pip's, looking more interested than alarmed. She looked like she wanted to pick them apart and see how they worked. The hedgewitch was a little bit Empty herself, Eleanor reflected. Cut off from caring. It was part of what made her powerful. They should all try to be like that. Then Otto wouldn't look pale and shaky, and Pip wouldn't have tear tracks raking through the dirt on her cheeks. They could have waited calmly and patiently for Eleanor to arrive.

"What are you doing with *them*?" Pip demanded.

"They are going to help us escape. And they're going to come with us. Trust me," Eleanor said, and Pip nodded. *Pip should have asked a lot more questions,* Eleanor reflected. If she'd been properly Empty, she wouldn't have just let Eleanor tell her what to do.

"Do you have the keys?" Otto asked, swallowing his discomfort.

"No, but I can make them," Melia said. "I will need to borrow from each of you to do it. It will be very uncomfortable, but please submit."

"Whoa. Hold up. What are you going to do to us?" Pip asked. Eleanor would have been irritated, if she could feel irritation. Couldn't Pip see that they were doing what they needed to?

Actually, she *was* irritated. And then, very faintly, alarmed. The Emptying was wearing off already! If it wore off too much, the Empty at the door might sense them and come to investigate why there were suddenly extra people down below.

"They can make things out of emotions and stuff," Eleanor said. "It's just borrowing. She can put them back. Right?"

"If I make a physical object, I can unmake it and return what I took," Melia confirmed.

"Start with me," the hedgewitch said. "I'm curious about the process."

Melia nodded and drifted down the aisle to the hedgewitch's cell. She reached out and put her fingertips to the hedgewitch's temples, and the hedgewitch let out a little sigh.

Then Melia dropped her hands and opened her palm. In her left hand rested a long silver key. "Curiosity makes an excellent key," Melia said. The hedgewitch's eyes looked a tad dull, and she stared at Melia with a bored expression.

Melia opened the door. The hedgewitch stepped out. She looked like she wanted to ask a question but couldn't quite think of it. "Who is next?" Melia asked.

"Can't you just use that key for all of us?" Otto asked, equal parts wary and interested. The hedgewitch gave a gasp, and Otto frowned at her. "What's wrong? Does it still hurt?"

"It doesn't hurt," the hedgewitch answered.

"What *does* it feel like?" he asked, but she just stared at him.

"It's very hard to describe," Eleanor said.

"But how—" Otto started.

"We're running out of time," Ash said, cutting him off.

"Then I guess you'd better take my curiosity next," Otto said.

Melia walked over to him, but when she set her fingers to his temples she shook her head. "Your curiosity is . . . stuck. I will take this." She drew her hands away, the key forming in the air as she did. It was bubblegum pink and had a bubble wand on the end.

"What did you take for *that*?" Otto asked, peering at it.

"I want to get home to see my sisters," Melia said.

"Interesting. You're right, I don't anymore. Objectively speaking, they're pretty annoying," Otto said. Eleanor felt a tiny wiggle of amusement somewhere deep within her.

Something scraped behind her. She turned, but there was nothing—only the stone walls and the stairs back up. She frowned. What had that sound been?

A faint howl sounded, as if coming from very far away.

She shuddered. *The hounds.*

There was something wrong in the air. Like running your fingers over cloth and finding a snagged thread. She thought of Wander, stitching up the air to mend the tears she'd made by traveling the Wending. Had Eleanor left a tear behind as well?

Eleanor resisted the urge to tell Melia to hurry. Melia already knew she needed to move quickly. Rushing her wouldn't help. But once Pip was free—"Boredom hates a locked door"—Eleanor leaned in to whisper to her.

"Have Gloaming ready. The umbral hounds are near."

Pip nodded. Melia unmade the keys with a gesture, and Pip gave a shiver as the sliver of boredom slipped back into her.

The growling that Eleanor had heard earlier came again, closer this time. The hounds were close. She reached for the Wending—and found nothing. She frowned. She'd found it before. Why wasn't it there now? She reached again. This time, she felt it—the way between worlds. It was faint, but growing slowly brighter.

It wasn't the only faint thing. All the bright threads that joined her to the others had faded almost to nothing. All her connections to people. All the connections between worlds.

Come on, Wending, she thought. Her whole self was coming alive again, and any minute the Empty would sense her or the hounds would arrive.

"Now," Ash said, tearing her attention away. "How are you getting us all out of here?"

"I'm going to open something called the Wending," Eleanor said. "It will take us to another world. Hopefully the *right* one, this time."

"How?" Melia pressed. "Is it some spell?"

"No. It's just—well, me," Eleanor said.

"You can open the way between worlds yourself?" Melia asked sharply. "It's not an object or a spell or a potion. It's you."

"That's right," Eleanor said impatiently.

"Then you're the one we need," Melia said, her voice cold.

"What?" Otto said, alarmed.

"Melia?" Thea asked uncertainly.

"You will serve our parents and open the way to other worlds, so that our armies can spill across them and conquer them all," Melia said. Her voice was flat—no triumph. No guilt.

"What did you do?" Ash demanded.

"I played along to find the information I needed, like you should have," she replied.

"You told Mother and Father what we were doing," Ash said.

"They'll be here soon," Melia confirmed, as the others stared in horror.

"How could you?" Thea asked, eyes filling with tears.

Ash's voice was shaky. "I noticed it when we were making ourselves look Empty, but I thought I must have been mistaken. You've Emptied yourself, haven't you? What did you take?"

"The parts that hurt," Melia said. "I couldn't bear the things Mother made me do, Ash. It was the only way I could survive. It gave me clarity. Peace. You could have that, too."

Ash rounded on Eleanor. "Get us out of here. Now."

"I'm *trying*," Eleanor said, but the threads of the worlds were still slipping from her reach.

Pip let out a startled cry and pointed. Descending the stairs was the stretched-out figure of the Pallid King. He should have been too tall for the space, but the walls seemed to stretch around him. He folded his spidery hands and regarded Eleanor with those black eyes that did not catch the light.

"You see?" Melia said, turning to her father. "Your answer. We can use her to find and conquer other worlds. As I promised."

"*Bring her to me*," the Pallid King said in a whisper that skittered along Eleanor's skin.

"Don't you dare," said Pip, bringing Gloaming to bear. The Pallid King extended one long finger, pointing at her. Pip gasped. She dropped to one knee, Gloaming clanging against the floor as her arms went slack. Otto started forward, but the hedgewitch reached out and caught his arm, tugging him back with her, toward the far wall.

Ash stood between Eleanor and his father, his hands in fists at his sides. The Pallid King looked down at the two of them. She looked up and up and up at his towering figure, and discovered that her fear was finally returning.

Looking straight into the Pallid King's face was hard—like staring at a Wrong Thing. She'd been mistaken when she thought the monarchs didn't have faces. The Pallid King's face did have features, a nose and a cruel, downturned mouth. It was just that unless she was staring directly at it, she couldn't remember it even long enough to realize what she was seeing.

"*Move aside, my son*," the Pallid King whispered. Ash trembled. "*We admire your cleverness. Obey me now, and you will be forgiven. You will ride with us as we open the doors to many worlds. Yours will be the sword and the crown. Yours will be the throne.*"

The growling Eleanor had heard earlier grew louder. Turned to howling. The Pallid King looked toward the noise, frowning.

"*What—*"

The wall beside him ripped open, and the road came spilling out. The road, and Shatterblack and Rag-a-bone, their eyes blazing. They sailed through the air toward Eleanor.

The next few moments were complete chaos. The Pallid King roared in fury. The hounds, suddenly realizing their prey wasn't alone, launched themselves at the newly discovered threat. The Empty soldiers rushed to defend their king.

Eleanor whirled around. *Now or never,* she thought. *Come on, Wending.*

With all the hope and fear and power she had in her, she *reached.* And she found it. It was like the moment when you finally understand a tricky math problem. She almost laughed as the sense of the Wending unfolded in her mind. *Yes! Open a road. Take us home,* she thought, and shouted in triumph as the far wall, where Otto and the hedgewitch were sheltered, vanished. A cobbled road flowed past it—a very familiar cobbled road. It was Eden Eld.

"Go! Hurry!" she shouted. The hedgewitch needed no more prompting. Holding Otto firmly by the arm, she dragged him onto the newly appeared road.

Pip scrambled to her feet, the king's control failing. She glanced at the fight, and then at Thea, who stood frozen in terror, her back against the bars. Pip reached out a hand.

"Coming?" she asked, and the grin that stretched across her face was Jack, through and through. Rescuing the fair maiden. Pip and Thea ran onto the road. Eleanor started after them.

"*Stop her,*" the Pallid King whispered.

A hand clamped around her arm. She wheeled, nearly falling over as it yanked her to an abrupt stop. She stared into Ash's face. He stared back.

"Let's go," she said. She searched his eyes. He wasn't Empty. She could see the fear in them. "Ash, we can escape. Just let me go, and you can come with us."

"*Bring her here,*" the Pallid King commanded. The Empty now had the hounds at bay, driving them back up the stairs. One of the hounds gave a horrible, high-pitched yelp. Pip was shouting Eleanor's name, but it seemed to come from a great distance.

"Ash," Melia said. She stood at her father's side. Her face was stony. "Don't be a fool."

Ash's expression hardened. "I'm sorry," he said. His hand tightened around her arm.

The kitten-of-ashes suddenly burst out of Ash's shirt, sinking her tiny needle teeth into his earlobe.

Ash yelped, dropping Eleanor's arm as the kitten swung from his ear. He swiped at her and she fell to the floor with a yowl. Eleanor ducked and grabbed the kitten as Ash reared back, hand clapped to his bleeding, singed ear.

Eleanor ran. Pip reached out and grabbed her arm, pulling her onto the road.

"Close it!" Pip hollered.

Panting, exhausted, Eleanor turned. The Pallid King had withdrawn. His arm ended above the wrist. It looked more like splintered wood than flesh.

Close, close, close, she willed the road. It began to disentangle itself from the Pallid King's world. Ash walked toward the road, but he didn't step onto it. Eleanor couldn't read his expression. Was that anger, or guilt?

The last ribbon of connection was fading. In the instant before the dungeon vanished, Ash looked her straight in the eyes. "Keep Thea safe," he said.

"I promise," Eleanor replied.

And then he was gone.

Thirteen

Eleanor caught her breath. The dungeon was gone, but her fear was slow to fade. That whole debacle had taken less than five minutes, but it felt like an eternity.

"Where are we?" Thea asked quietly.

"Eden Eld," Otto answered.

"It's where we're from," Eleanor added in response to the girl's puzzled expression. The cobblestone road was one of the ones downtown, where all the shops were decorated to look quaint and old-timey and the streetlights looked like Victorian gas lamps. It was night now, and the lamps glowed with pale, colorless light through a thin fog. There wasn't anyone around, but that wasn't unusual.

"Um. Guys?" Pip said. "We have a problem."

She was looking up into the sky. Eleanor frowned and followed her gaze—and her heart skipped a beat. She'd thought it was the middle of the night because it was dark out. But the sun was still in the sky.

It was just covered by the moon.

"The eclipse," Otto whispered. The faintest line of light licked the edge of the moon, marking its position in the sky. "It's still totality. How is that possible? Did we come out in exactly the same moment we left?"

"Time does work differently in the Wending," the hedge-witch said, but she sounded doubtful. "Was it this cold when you left?"

Eleanor shivered. The air was brisk and chilly, no hint of the early summer warmth they'd left behind. And the leaves on the trees had fallen. They were scattered across the cobblestones.

And they were gray.

"This doesn't make any sense," Eleanor whispered. "How is it still the eclipse?"

A little hiccup of sadness drew Eleanor's attention. Thea stood off to the side under the glow of a streetlamp, shoulders hunched, holding the kitten-of-ashes cradled in her arms. The kitten looked ruffled and very annoyed at her ill-treatment, but Eleanor didn't think she was hurt.

Eleanor knelt down in front of Thea. "I'm sorry about your brother and sister," she said.

"Why would they do that?" Thea asked plaintively. Fat, glistening tears ran down her cheeks.

"Mr. January betrayed us. Big surprise," Pip growled. She kicked a rock, sending it plinking into the side of the café they stood in front of. Its windows, Eleanor saw with growing alarm, were boarded up.

"Why are you comforting her? She is your enemy. You ought to dispatch her before she grows wise enough and powerful enough to realize it," the hedgewitch said.

"She's a little kid," Eleanor said, putting herself between the hedgewitch and the trembling Thea.

"What she is *now* matters less than what she will *become*," the hedgewitch countered. "We should eliminate her."

"Whoa! Nobody's eliminating anyone! Especially not kids!" Pip said. "I don't know what kind of creepy nonsense is happening, but if Eleanor says she's on our side, she's on our side." Pip went to stand next to Eleanor, arms folded.

"Why did she say I'm your enemy? Who is Mr. January?" Thea asked, looking confused.

Eleanor sighed. "It's hard to explain," she said. They'd brought Thea into the present—did that mean there was no Katie Rhodes here? Or did it mean they had Katie Rhodes *and* Thea in this timeline? Her brain felt itchy thinking about it.

"It's so quiet," Otto said, sounding troubled. "And the moon should be moving. It's staying completely still. That doesn't make any sense."

"Let's see if we can find anyone to explain what the heck is going on," Eleanor said.

"Good idea," Otto agreed. But as soon as Eleanor took a step, her legs gave out. She collapsed with a groan, catching herself on her palms. Otto and Pip ran to her, helping her back up. She leaned heavily against Pip, and she could feel her eyelids starting to drag.

"I'm sorry. Just . . . really tired," she said.

"You've opened the Wending twice, dragged me across a half-dozen worlds, and escaped the throne room without a proper rest," the hedgewitch said. "Of course you're exhausted."

Eleanor wished she could convince herself there was even a hint of motherly concern in her voice. "I'm fine," she grated out.

"You're really not," Otto told her. "Look, there's a bench. Sit down. Rest."

Eleanor wanted to object, but she was too tired. She let Pip guide her over to the bench, and she sank down onto it.

"You four stay here. I'll look around," the hedgewitch said.

Pip snorted. "Because that worked out so well last time. I'll come with you."

"I don't need a child for protection," the hedgewitch said, brow arched.

"I am no mere child. I am the warrior, or have you forgotten?" Pip asked in her warrior voice, hand on Gloaming's hilt.

The hedgewitch waved a hand. "Fine. Come, then, brave guardian."

"Let us go hence, and see if the burrito place on Third is open," Pip declared. They strode off together.

Thea climbed up on the bench next to Eleanor. The kitten-of-ashes jumped free and perched on the edge of the bench, looking around with bright, curious eyes.

"Who is Mr. January?" Thea asked again.

Eleanor looked at Otto, who shrugged. Eleanor wasn't sure what was best to tell Thea—what to leave out, what to reveal, what would hurt her, what would frighten her. So she settled on the easiest thing: the truth.

"When we came to your kingdom, we didn't just travel between worlds. We traveled to the past," she explained. Thea's eyes were wide, but she didn't interrupt. So Eleanor continued, though her explanation was halting, fragmented. Otto jumped in when she faltered. Thea didn't ask any questions. She didn't say a single word until the very end.

Thea looked away, down the dark street. "Mother and Father must have found a way out of our world, eventually. And conquered all those worlds they talked about. I wonder how they did it."

Eleanor had a bad feeling she knew the answer to that. Katie Rhodes was the mistress of the Wending. She knew how to open the way between worlds. Eleanor would bet that she was the one who'd eventually figured it out for her parents.

"But people fought back," Otto said. "They locked the Pallid Kingdom away completely. The People Who Look Away—uh, that is . . ."

"Me and my brother and sister, you mean," Thea said softly. "We did all those horrible things to you to let Mother and Father back out. Even though we hated them."

"The People Who Look Away are very, very old," Eleanor said. "Centuries old. A lot can happen in hundreds of years."

"Does it have to?" Thea asked. She looked at Eleanor pleadingly. "Do I have to be wicked? Or can I stay me?"

"We won't let anything happen to you," Eleanor pledged, taking her hand. "You don't have to be anything you don't want to be."

"Maybe," Otto said. Eleanor gave him a withering look. He spread his hands. "I'm just saying, we don't know how any of this works. Maybe it's her destiny to be evil. Or maybe not! We just changed the past. Who *knows* what that's going to do!"

"Weird, weird things," Pip said. Eleanor sat up, startled by her approach. The hedgewitch was with her, looking grim.

"You'd better come see this," the hedgewitch said.

Eleanor got to her feet. Her legs still felt like rubber, but the rest had helped. Thea took her hand as they followed the hedgewitch and Pip down the street to the town square.

"So," Otto said mildly, "does anyone remember there being a giant statue of Mr. January in the middle of town?"

The statue had to be twelve feet tall. It showed what could only be Mr. January—he had his cane, his formal clothes, his smirk. It had been designed so that there were two Mr. Januarys looking both forward and back, merged at the middle.

"'In honor of our beloved mayor,'" Otto read from the plaque on the base of the statue.

"What is going *on* here?" Eleanor asked, aghast.

Movement caught her eye. She turned just in time to see someone ducking inside a shop. She looked around again, slowly. Here and there, she could see faces peering out at them from behind curtains and between blinds.

Claws clicked on cobblestones behind them. Eleanor turned with a gasp, expecting the umbral hounds. But it wasn't them.

It was the graveyard dog.

Mr. January's hulking beast of a dog was advancing down the street toward them, ears pricked forward, breath huffing out in great plumes of smoke.

"You," he rumbled. "Was looking for you. Found you."

A new sound joined the steady *click-click-click* of his claws: a sound like tumbling stones. A fresh cobblestone path rippled through the square, coming to meet the street they stood beside. Rag-a-bone and Shatterblack streamed down it, their tongues lolling and eyes bright.

"Leave them!" Rag-a-bone cried.

"They're ours to catch!" Shatterblack added.

"Back off," the graveyard dog barked. "I smelled them first."

The three dogs glared at each other. Then turned, as one, toward the humans.

"We should probably run," Otto whispered.

A car engine revved down the street. Pip reached for her sword. The dogs charged.

A van whipped around the corner so fast it almost lifted off its wheels. It blasted past the dogs, sending them yelping and scrambling in all directions, and screeched to a halt in front of them, cutting them off momentarily.

The driver rolled down the window, and Eleanor let out a shaky breath of relief. "Uncle Ben?"

"Get in, quick!" he said, motioning frantically.

Eleanor didn't waste time asking questions. She hauled open the back door and helped Thea up. The others piled in behind. They'd hardly closed the door behind them when Ben slammed on the gas, throwing them back against the seats in an ungainly tangle. Eleanor twisted to look out the back window. The dogs were falling behind quickly. Shatterblack and Rag-a-bone snapped at the graveyard dog's flanks, slowing them all down even more. Eleanor let out a relieved sigh and turned back around.

Only then did she notice that the floor of the van was papered with flyers for missing people. Some of them Eleanor didn't recognize, but there were a few kids from school and people she knew around town, and—

Jenny and Naomi. "Aunt Jenny and Naomi are missing?" Eleanor said, picking up the flyer. She recognized the photo—it was on the mantel at home. "What happened? Uncle Ben, what's going on?"

"I kind of hoped you might know, since you've been missing, too," Ben said. He'd slowed down a bit as they left the town proper, but he was still hurtling along at well over the speed limit. Ben was the most cautious driver Eleanor knew, other than Jack, but now she clutched the door to keep steady as he swayed in the lane.

Eleanor looked at him in the rearview mirror. He was scruffy—well, scruffier than usual, not in his usual "friendly forest bear" way—and he was wearing a battered baseball cap over long, scraggly hair.

"Wait. How long have we been gone?" Eleanor asked.

"Since the eclipse started," Ben said.

"And that was . . ." Eleanor began.

"Four months ago," Ben said.

Eleanor sat back with a moan. How could they have been gone four months?

"Wait. *What day is it?*" Pip demanded.

"Well, let's see. It's hard to keep track without the days and nights, but it's what, two a.m.? So that means it's officially October thirtieth," Ben said.

Eleanor, Pip, and Otto looked at each other in silent horror. For a long moment none of them said a word.

It was October 30. Tomorrow was Halloween.

And Mr. January would be coming for them.

Fourteen

Ben pulled up in front of the house and threw the van into park, making it lurch. "Things have been gray like this since the eclipse started. That's also when people started going missing, and *that* happened." He gestured out past the house. It was hard to tell in the perpetual dark, but as Eleanor squinted, she realized that beyond the orchard, the pine trees that surrounded Eden Eld weren't there. There was only a solid wall of gray.

Ben waved toward the house. "It's better inside the house. We'll be safe in there."

Ben ushered them all in and slammed the door shut. As soon as they crossed the threshold, their color returned. Everything inside the house looked normal, too—the house had magical protections on it that had kept the gray from encroaching every time the People Who Look Away came after them. Ben threw the locks—all nine of them, bolted along the door from top to bottom. Only then did he let out a breath and relax, his shoulders sagging.

"I think you'd better tell us what is going on here," Eleanor said, as kindly as she could. Ben looked like he was barely holding things together.

"I should tell you? How about you tell me?" Ben said. He was a big man, and his voice was loud and wild, but somehow it all made him seem very small. "You three. You disappeared," he said, pointing at Eleanor, Otto, and Pip. Then he looked at the hedgewitch. "And Claire? You're dead or a criminal or something! I don't know who the kid is, but she looks like she got lost on her way to a Renaissance festival, so she's not really upping the normal quotient here." He gave a manic laugh and swept his baseball cap from his head, running his hand over his hair.

"Uncle Ben, I know this is strange, but I promise it's going to be okay," Eleanor said, putting a hand on his arm. He flinched away. She dropped her hand, stung. Was he afraid of her?

It didn't matter. Soon he'd forget that anything strange was happening. That's what had happened all the other times he'd brushed up against the Wrong Things.

Usually it started working sooner than this, though. "Nothing is okay," he said, sounding lost. "Jenny and Naomi are gone. The January Society has everyone living in terror, and *he's* here, and we haven't heard anything from the outside world in months. How is any of that okay?"

"Let's go sit down," Eleanor said. She reached for Ben's hand, and this time he didn't flinch away. "Come on. I'll make you some cocoa." She patted the back of his hand and led him through the crowd of her companions.

"Maybe you could go check the perimeter?" she suggested to the hedgewitch delicately. Eleanor wasn't sure which would alarm him more—talking to her mother, who he thought burned her house down, or talking to a totally different person who had her face.

"I'll make sure the wards on this place are still in working order," the hedgewitch said with a nod. "Perhaps you would like to come with me, Thea."

Eleanor stiffened. "I don't think that's a good idea," she said.

The hedgewitch huffed. "I promise you she's safe with me. For now," she said. "And I need to check her over to make sure there is no way her brother can sense her here."

"Swear you won't hurt her," Pip said, narrowing her eyes.

"I swear on the Stories and on my own life," the hedgewitch said with exaggerated patience. "Good enough for you?"

Eleanor looked at Thea. The girl gave a tiny, almost imperceptible nod. The hedgewitch put her hand out, and Thea took it. Eleanor watched as they walked away, stomach pinched. She didn't know if she trusted the hedgewitch, but she didn't think she'd actually hurt a little girl.

Eleanor led Ben down the hall to the kitchen. Having gotten them into the house, he now seemed to have lost all direction, and let her guide him to a chair. She surveyed the kitchen with dismay. There were boxes of crackers and cookies and bags of chips open everywhere. Empty cans were piled into a mountain, spilling over the sides of the recycling bin, and while the dishes had been washed, they were all stacked high on the drying rack, threatening to topple.

If the world outside Eden Eld was swallowed by gray, how did they have fresh groceries? Eleanor opened the fridge with trepidation, but she was relieved to find it well stocked. There was a gallon of milk on the top shelf. She checked the expiration date. It just read NEVER ☺.

She frowned and looked at the label. It showed a picture of a farmer facing away from the viewer, standing next to an inexplicably menacing cow. JANUARY DAIRY, it read.

"Is that safe to drink?" Pip asked, looking over her shoulder.

"Ben's still alive," Eleanor pointed out. "And judging by the recycling, he's had lots of it."

She got up on a chair to reach the good cocoa on the highest shelf of the cupboard and then heated it on the stove. She wanted to ask a million questions, but she waited until she had closed Ben's fingers around the mug of cocoa.

"All right, Uncle Ben. Why don't you tell us what's happened since the eclipse?" Eleanor said gently.

Ben took a long, loud slurp of cocoa, wiped his lips with his hand (making Otto grimace), and began. "We were going outside to look at the eclipse. Jack ran outside. Then there was this woman there. She had these glittering things floating around her."

"Wander," Eleanor said.

He shrugged. "She grabbed Jack's hand and suddenly there was this *hole* in the air, and they jumped through. Then everything got dark. I heard Jenny say my name, but when I turned around, she was just . . . gone. They both were." A sob rose in his chest. He swallowed it down. "I was frantic. Calling their names. Running all over the place. It took me a while to realize that the eclipse . . . it wasn't going away. And you were gone, too. After that, things got strange."

"They weren't already?" Otto muttered.

Ben took another swig of cocoa. "Jenny and Naomi weren't the only ones missing. A whole bunch of people were. Only they weren't just *missing.* All their things were gone, too. Naomi's room is completely empty. Jenny's paintings are gone. It's the same all over town. They're still in photographs, but all other evidence that they ever existed in the first place has been wiped. And then people that *shouldn't* be here started showing up."

"You said the January Society was here," Eleanor said. The January Society had been sucked into the gray world on Halloween. She looked over at Pip. Pip's mother had been part of the January Society—she'd been in *charge* of it. And she'd tried to give them to Mr. January on Halloween. Did this mean she was back? Pip must be frantic. But her expression was simply focused and curious.

Ben nodded. "They work for the mayor. This weird guy came out of the gray and said that he was here to save us. But if you ask me, he doesn't know what's going on any better than the rest of us." He stared down into his cup, a foam of chocolatey milk striping his mustache. "But you're back. So maybe everyone else will come back, too. Maybe all of this will end."

"He's not forgetting," Pip noted, staring intently at Ben.

"I guess this is just too big to forget," Eleanor said.

"Sometimes it gets hard to think," Ben confessed. He put a hand to his head, wagging it side to side. "Like everything gets scrambled, and you have to remember all over again. But you get used to it."

"Where do all the groceries come from?" Eleanor asked. "How is there even still power?"

"Eden Eld is perfect," Ben said with a stretched-out, plastered-on grin. "The stores are always stocked. The lights never go out. No one gets sick and *no one leaves.*" He laughed horribly, a sound that choked off into a sob. Eleanor fought back a wave of fear. Why was this happening?

She was very, very afraid that the answer was *because of me.*

"What about my family?" Otto asked. "Are they missing?"

"What about my dad?" Pip added.

Ben ran a hand over his head. "Pip, your dad disappeared with the others. So did Lily."

Otto moaned. Lily was one of his three younger sisters—triplets.

"We'll get them back," Eleanor told him fiercely.

"My poor parents," Otto said, his eyes distant. "Losing me and Lily at the same time. And Gina and May—they must be so scared."

Eleanor pulled him close to her, squeezing him tight. Otto's first thought was how scared and sad his family was. He was always thinking about other people. But he wouldn't always. The hedgewitch Story would steal that, too.

"Should we call them? Do the phones work?" Pip asked.

"They work," Ben said. "That's how I knew you were in town. Mr. Clarkson called to warn me. We can give your family a call and let them know you're okay, Otto."

Otto, sniffling, pulled himself away from Eleanor. "No. I'm glad they're safe, but we shouldn't tell them I'm back. If Mr. January gets us or the Story . . . if I . . ." He slumped. "If they have to lose me, it's better if they only lose me once, right?"

Eleanor took his hand. Her heart ached for him—and for his parents, and his sisters, too young to even begin to understand what was happening.

There was a scrape from the hallway. The locks on the front door were opening, one by one. Pip leaped up with alarm, but Ben gave them a calming wave of his hand.

"That's just Barry," he said.

"Who's Barry?" Eleanor asked.

"My roommate. This is technically his house," Ben said. There was the sound of the door opening and clomping footsteps coming into the hall, and Ben called out, "In the kitchen. We've got visitors."

Eleanor was so tired and her brain was so full that she heard *Barry* and *his house* and couldn't make sense of it at all. And so when Bartimaeus Ashford, one of the thirteen founders of

Eden Eld, stepped into the room, all she could do was stare blankly.

He stared right back. "This is unexpected," he said.

The last time they'd seen Bartimaeus was on Halloween. Pip and Eleanor had found the secret room in the clock tower where he'd hidden himself away for decades. Before that, he'd built this house and collected all the artifacts it was stocked with. He was also the one who'd written *Thirteen Tales of the Gray.* He was a tall, creaky man, with a fluff of white hair on his head and the kind of glasses you mostly wear so that you can peer over them disapprovingly. The vest and suit jacket he was wearing looked almost exactly the same as the ones he'd had on Halloween, though a bit more worn out.

"What are you doing here?" Eleanor demanded, rising.

"Who is he?" Otto asked. That's right—Otto hadn't been with them when they met Bartimaeus. He'd been captured by the January Society.

"You know each other?" Ben asked.

"Bartimaeus Ashford, Otto. Otto, Bartimaeus," Eleanor said. "Now back to my question."

"My sanctuary in the clock tower is currently inaccessible," he said, in the detached tone Eleanor remembered from their first encounter, like none of this had anything to do with him. "Your uncle was generous enough to allow me to take up residence in my former abode."

"So you finally had to stop lurking around not helping anyone?" Pip asked.

"You keep insisting that I've done nothing to help, but that's simply not true. I've done a great deal, including building this house, with all its protections. And doing quite a bit of work for your father, young Eleanor, not that he's ever bothered to come back and thank me for it," Bartimaeus said, and, as anticipated, peered over his glasses with a scowl.

"He was in an enchanted sleep for thirteen years," Eleanor said defensively. "You might have *told* me that Jack was my father."

"And what could you possibly have done with that information, other than distract yourself into certain doom?" Bartimaeus asked. "You were rather focused on other things."

"That didn't stop you from telling me to give him a message. Not very useful when I didn't even know his name," Eleanor said, rolling her eyes. Then she gasped. "Yes!"

"Yes what?" Otto asked.

Eleanor pointed at Bartimaeus. "That's the message he told me to deliver. He said to tell my father the answer was 'yes.' *Jack* told us the question was 'Can I get rid of the Prime Stories?'"

"The what?" Ben said, looking baffled.

"That wasn't his precise phrasing, but yes, that's accurate," Bartimaeus said. He seemed to notice Gloaming for the first time, then blinked at Eleanor. "My goodness. The Stories have moved on, haven't they?"

Eleanor nodded. "But you can tell us how to stop them. How to get rid of them. So? How do we do it?"

"Is this really the most urgent question right now?" Pip asked.

"With our luck, he's going to disappear again and we won't see him until *next* Halloween. If we're even still alive," Eleanor pointed out. She glared at Bartimaeus. "So talk."

"Really? Now?" Bartimaeus asked.

"You heard the lady," Pip said.

"Spill," Otto added, doing his best to look intimidating. He managed "exhausted and cranky," at least.

"I believe the answer lies in the Library of Endersea," Bartimaeus said.

"The who?" Ben asked.

Eleanor frowned. Where had she heard that before? Wander had mentioned it. And so had Thea. "That's the library that contains every story from every world, right?"

"That's the one. It is famously impossible to reach. So impossible that I hesitated to even mention it to your father. But *you* . . ."

"We have the Wending," Eleanor said. Bartimaeus nodded. Ben looked between them, sighed, and seemed to give up on trying to understand any of it. "You think that the Library can somehow help us?"

"My research suggests that the Prime Stories—the *actual*, physical originals of the tales that have possessed you—are in the Library's collection. If you destroy them, their hold on you will end," Bartimaeus said.

"But the Stories aren't books, are they? They're in us," Otto said, frowning.

Bartimaeus harrumphed. He gestured in the air with one hand, like a lecturing professor. "Stories in the wild are mercurial things, constantly changing. Put one of *them* in a person and it changes to match them, doing no harm at all. Stories like the ones attached to the three of you have to keep their shape. And for that, they have to be written down in books."

"Hey, I mean, you can destroy a book," Ben said, clearly lost but trying to help.

"You can absolutely destroy a book," Eleanor said, cracking her knuckles.

"If you can get past the Librarian," Bartimaeus said.

"Naturally," Ben said, nodding.

"Then we're going to the Library of Endersea," Eleanor said, and felt a heavy burden drop from her shoulders. There was a way out of this.

"No, we're not," Pip cut in. "Eleanor, have you looked around? There's a permanent eclipse in the sky! People are vanishing! Mr. January's going to come for us *tomorrow*! We do not have time to be worrying about the Stories right now. Besides—without them, we're weaker. We need them."

Eleanor crossed her arms, matching her stubborn glare for stubborn glare. "We beat Mr. January without the Stories before."

"Barely. And he's had a whole year to think up new tricks," Pip said.

"But we did it. We didn't have powers or a magical sword. We had an old walking stick and good ideas," Eleanor reminded her. "We need to get that thing out of you before—"

"I'm the one who gets to decide that!" Pip snapped. "They're my memories. It's my life."

"But it's not just you anymore," Eleanor said. "And even if it *was*, we would still help you, because you're our friend, and we don't want to lose you!" Her voice rose until she was almost yelling, her hands balled up into fists at her sides. How could Pip be so stubborn? Did she *want* to forget them?

"I'm not getting rid of the warrior," Pip said, shouting just as loudly as Eleanor. "Not until you're safe! Not until my dad is safe and the triplets are safe and everyone is *safe*, which they can't be until I *win*!"

"Until *we* win," Otto said quietly. Pip looked at him, panting a little, her hair sticking to her face. "You aren't on your own, Pip."

"I know. Sometimes it feels like I am, though," she whispered.

"Yeah," Otto said. "I know what you mean."

Ben, who had been looking rapidly between them as they spoke, stepped forward. Wordlessly, he wrapped Pip up in a one-armed hug. With the other, he grabbed Eleanor—then reached out and snagged the collar of Otto's shirt, yanking him in. "You kids," he said roughly, and his voice broke. "I had no idea what you were dealing with. You are amazing. All of you."

For a moment they stood there, leaning into Ben's comforting warmth. Then Pip pulled away, swiping a hand over her face to hide a sniffle. "I'm just saying," she said, her voice cracking, "we have other things we need to deal with first. Starting with finding out what's wrong with Eden Eld."

"I should think that would be obvious by now," the hedgewitch said, entering with Thea in tow. "*You* are." She looked right at Eleanor.

"Me?" Eleanor said, brow wrinkling.

"You and your careless, graceless tearing through the Wending. You have no skill, no precision. You fling your will at it without focus, and it picks up everything you're thinking. You wanted more time and you were thinking about the People Who Look Away, so it flung you into the past and right into their path, and dragged me along with you. Then you ripped Thea out of her time, demanding it take you back to Eden Eld—only which Eden Eld? The one you're constantly obsessed over. The Eden Eld of Halloween. It's only doing what your thoughts tell it to, because you haven't bothered to control them," the hedgewitch said. "Oh. Hello, Bartimaeus."

"Hedgewitch," Bartimaeus said uncomfortably, shifting somewhat nervously from one foot to the other. She gave him an unimpressed look.

"You're still alive, then."

"Indeed." He cleared his throat. "You say this girl was taken from the past? And the Wending, it was opened from here in Eden Eld? Then the hedgewitch is right—that does explain the eclipse. Time has fractured, and the fracture is centered here, on Eden Eld. My goodness. Using the Wending without training is dangerous enough. You never know which whim it might pluck from your mind."

Eleanor quailed. "All of this is my fault? I . . . broke time? I brought us straight to Halloween?" They'd lost months to plan and prepare. They'd lost Jenny and Naomi and Lily and Pip's dad and who knew how many other people. And it was her fault.

"We broke time. That's . . . kind of epic," Otto said. Eleanor and Pip looked at him. He spread his hands. "*Bad,* obviously. But also epic."

"Can we fix it?" Ben asked hopefully. "Can we bring everyone back?"

"If you returned the girl to her time—" Bartimaeus started.

"No," all three of them snapped at him.

Eleanor set her jaw. "We'll find a way to fix things *and* save Thea," she said.

"Okay. But . . . how?" Otto pressed. He looked at Pip. She looked at Eleanor.

Eleanor sighed. "I have no idea."

Fifteen

Eleanor woke up in her bed, and for one blissful moment she didn't remember how she got there. Then she rolled over and spotted the eclipse outside the window. She groaned and sat up. How long had she been asleep? She and the others had sat up for a long time, talking to Bartimaeus and the hedgewitch about ways to fix time. At some point Eleanor had started drifting off, and Ben had insisted everyone under the age of a hundred go get some sleep.

Eleanor slipped out of bed. Thea was asleep in the armchair by her desk, a blanket tucked over her. Pip and Otto were passed out on the floor in sleeping bags. There were plenty of rooms in the house, but none of them had wanted to sleep alone. Eleanor stole out into the hall, not wanting to wake them, and crept downstairs. Her stomach was rumbling. She didn't really like the idea of eating Mr. January's weird groceries, but if the alternative was starving, she'd give them a try.

She found the hedgewitch in the kitchen, clearing away the trash and putting away the dishes. "Is housework part of your Story?" Eleanor asked dryly as she padded in.

The hedgewitch gave her an amused look. "No, but orderliness is always helpful for my work. You don't want to add the wrong herb and end up with a poison instead of a love potion."

"Good point," Eleanor said. She moved to help, putting the dishes away in the dusty cupboards. They worked in silence for a few minutes.

"You and your friends are extremely resourceful," the hedgewitch said. "And wise beyond your years, and brave, and clever. All the things we ought to be." Her voice sounded distant. There was almost, Eleanor thought, a hint of sadness in it.

"You mean the things the Stories are supposed to be, right?" Eleanor asked, turning a mug by its handle until it was arranged in just the right way. *The way Aunt Jenny liked it,* she thought with a small pang.

"It seems cruel, that I have come into myself fully only at the very end of my time as the hedgewitch," the witch said. She stood looking out the kitchen window, but her eyes were unfocused. "It's a wonder to be the hedgewitch. There's all this knowledge, just *there* when you reach for it. But it's not in your head. It doesn't belong to you, not until you reach out and take it. If I'd known the end was coming, I would have claimed so much more."

"Would have?" Eleanor asked. She didn't really need to ask. She knew what the hedgewitch was saying, and what it meant.

"You aren't the hedgewitch anymore. It's Otto now, isn't it?" she asked.

The hedgewitch—or whoever she was, now—nodded. "It happened in the dungeon, when Melia stole my curiosity. You cannot be the hedgewitch without curiosity."

Eleanor sucked in a breath and looked away. Otto was going to begin to lose his memory. He was going to start to change. But worse than that, for all that she'd stopped seeing her mother in the hedgewitch's face, there had been some tiny part of her that still stubbornly believed that when she stopped being the hedgewitch, she would go back to just being *Mom*.

The woman standing in front of her was still a stranger. Her memories wouldn't be coming back. She would never be Eleanor's mother again.

"What are we supposed to call you, then?" Eleanor asked, voice harsh and unkind. "You really should have come up with a proper name."

"You could call me Claire, I suppose," she said, shrugging.

"No," Eleanor said, more firmly than she'd intended. The hedgewitch raised an eyebrow.

"That's fair. Something else, then." She sighed. "It isn't my fault, you know. What happened to your mother."

"It's the Story's fault, and you're the Story," Eleanor replied stubbornly.

"The Story is the thing that changes us and makes us, but we're merely one telling of it."

Eleanor didn't reply. It didn't matter whether the hedgewitch meant to take her mother away. All that mattered was that her mother was gone, and there was a hole in Eleanor's heart where she had been. She was going to lose them all. Her mother. Pip. Otto. And then she was going to lose even the *memory* of them, and that seemed like the most horrible thing of all.

The hedgewitch frowned, looking out into the orchard. "We have a visitor," she said.

"A visitor?" Eleanor peered past the hedgewitch's shoulder, and then she laughed. "This should be interesting," she said. She walked to the back door and opened it for their guest, who trotted in without so much as a hello and leaped up onto the kitchen counter.

"I thought those humans in town had all lost their kibbles, but here you are in the flesh," said the cat-of-ashes, magnificent tail swishing. "How did you manage that?"

"Ever hear of the Wending?" Eleanor asked.

The cat-of-ashes narrowed her eyes. "Pah. You're the ones that messed with time, then. I wouldn't have thought you—what is *that*?" She leaped to her feet so fast a cutting board went spinning off the counter and crashed to the floor. Her tail poofed into a bottlebrush.

The kitten-of-ashes stiff-legged into the kitchen. She arched her back and laid her ears flat against her skull, hissing and spitting sparks. Eleanor scooped up the furious kitten, shushing her with scratches behind the ears. The little feline hunkered into her arms and growled.

"She's the kitten-of-ashes," Eleanor said meekly. The cats looked at each other in unconcealed horror.

"It's *me*. But it's *small*. And weak and stupid," the cat-of-ashes said in a complaining tone. "Why would you bring that thing in here?"

"We helped the kitten-of-ashes and Thea escape the Pallid Kingdom," Eleanor said.

"Thea," the cat-of-ashes repeated. Her pupils had expanded to swallow her bright green irises, and she stretched her claws out almost nervously. "You stole a baby monster from the nest? You're bigger fools than I thought."

"Old," the kitten-of-ashes squeaked.

"I—I am not—how dare—" The cat-of-ashes stammered to a halt and began furiously grooming herself. Her voice came out garbled between fierce licks, muttering as if talking to herself. "Whiskerless fools. Meddling with things they shouldn't. What were they thinking?"

"Thea hated it there," Eleanor said. The kitten-of-ashes clambered its way up onto her shoulder, hunkering down under her hair and glowering at the older cat. "She's sleeping upstairs. I don't know what happens to her after we leave the Wending, but for now, she's with us." She said this with a hard look at the hedgewitch.

The hedgewitch crossed her arms. "I'm in agreement with the cat. It is an unnecessary risk to have her with us, and a missed opportunity. She'll turn on us eventually."

"I don't think she will," Eleanor objected. "She's just a little girl. If we take care of her, she'll have a chance to be good."

"You're the one who is going to suffer the most if you are wrong," the hedgewitch said. "The People Who Look Away don't need me, they need you."

"Then why do you even care?" Eleanor demanded. "You don't remember me. You don't care about me at all."

"I'm not *entirely* unfeeling. I don't *want* something bad to happen to you, Elle, and—" She stopped. Eleanor stared at her. *Elle.* Her mother had called her that. The hedgewitch tensed.

"Well, this is very dramatic," the cat-of-ashes said, looking a bit uncomfortable. "I suppose it explains where Katie got to, at least. And good riddance. Apart from the bit where it destroyed reality itself, it was a genius move."

"Wait," Eleanor said slowly. "If taking Thea made Katie disappear, how are you and the kitten-of-ashes both here?"

The cat and kitten wore identical smug expressions. "I'm a *cat.* I don't play by the rules," the cat-of-ashes drawled. She stretched. "Oh, I nearly forgot—the January Society is on its way."

"On their way here? Now?" Eleanor yelped. "Why didn't you say anything?"

"I was a bit distracted by figuring out how you had all gotten here. And then *that* showed up. How's a feline supposed to focus under these circumstances?" the cat-of-ashes demanded, flicking an irritated ear in the kitten's direction.

Eleanor swore under her breath and dashed toward the Great Room, scooping up the kitten-of-ashes on her way. Bartimaeus and Ben were in there, midway through a game of Catan.

"Longest road! Hand it over!" Ben declared, putting out his hand.

"The January Society is coming!" Eleanor interrupted. "We have to hide. Where's the key to the secret room?"

Bartimaeus looked over his glasses at her. "Have you not been paying attention? There is no secret room. All my between-world spaces collapsed."

"What's going on?" Pip asked sleepily, stepping into the room wearing Eleanor's pink flannel unicorn pajamas, Gloaming belted around her hips. Otto and Thea trailed after, looking mildly more awake.

"The January Society is coming," Eleanor said.

Just then, someone hammered on the door. "Should we hide?" Otto asked.

"They already know we're here. Better to face them unafraid," Pip said. The knocking came again.

"I'll get it," Ben said grimly, and strode toward the foyer. There was the sound of voices speaking quickly, Ben's tone one of protest, and then Delilah Foster walked into the Great Room. Ben trailed behind.

Eleanor hadn't seen Ms. Foster up close since Halloween, but she hadn't changed at all, from her immaculately tailored navy suit to the bright red nail polish she wore to the way she moved when she walked, like she was hunting something.

Of all the people to pop back into existence, did it have to be Delilah Foster?

Eleanor reached instinctively for Pip's hand, but Pip was looking at her mother with wariness, not distress, her hand on Gloaming's hilt.

Ms. Foster's eyes widened when she entered, and her perfect poise wobbled for a moment. "My goodness. It is true," she said, soft as the slithering of a snake. "All three of you. And is that—*Claire Barton*?" She stared at the hedgewitch with unconcealed shock and distaste.

"You are not welcome here," Bartimaeus rumbled. He looked thin and frail, standing before Delilah Foster with her bright colors and youthful face.

"Pip. *Darling*. It is so *wonderful* to see you," Delilah said, her smile wide and unconvincing. She held out her arms as if for Pip to rush into them.

"You're . . . my mother," Pip said. There was a small, puzzled line between her brows.

"Of course I am, Philippa my dear," Delilah said. Her lipstick was the color of a bruise, and it made her teeth look impossibly white in contrast. "And I'm delighted to find you returned. Delighted and—well, a bit confused. Perhaps you could explain it to me, Bartimaeus."

"I need not explain anything to you," Bartimaeus said. "Leave my house and leave me in peace."

"Defying Mr. January has serious consequences," Delilah said warningly.

He laughed. "What consequences would those be, Delilah? I was one of the original signatories to the deal. I enjoy all the same protections as Eden Eld itself."

"Not for long," she snapped, her voice bitter. "Without your little hidey-holes, time is going to catch up to you. No more keeping yourself alive. You're going to get old and weak."

"At this point, that will be an invigorating change of pace," Bartimaeus said, unperturbed. Eleanor smirked. She didn't exactly *like* Bartimaeus. He'd done the absolute bare minimum to help them, instead of actually putting himself in any risk to right the wrongs he'd helped cause. But she did enjoy seeing Ms. Foster flustered, as she looked between all of them.

The hedgewitch's hand fell to Eleanor's shoulder, almost possessively. Eleanor stiffened at the touch.

"Delilah. Things have changed since we last met, and you will find that I am not so easy to chase off," the hedgewitch said, her voice low and dangerous. "Claire Barton is gone. I am the hedgewitch, and these children are under my protection. When last we met, you nearly got burned. I promise you the fire will not be so easy to escape again."

Ms. Foster flinched, and Eleanor's breath caught. She was talking about the day their house burned down. The day that Eleanor's mother disappeared.

"Do you remember what happened on Halloween?" Eleanor asked. "Do you remember how we beat you, or did you get plucked from an earlier time? Do you want us to show you?"

Ms. Foster's lips thinned. "I have no idea how you three managed to wriggle out of the curse, but I promise you I won't let you do it again. I've been given a second chance," she said.

Eleanor peered at her. "Mr. January doesn't know you're here talking to us, does he?" Eleanor asked. Delilah's gaze snapped to her. "You wanted to find out what was going on before you told him. Because if we're here, maybe that means *you* messed up. And Mr. January wouldn't like that."

The hedgewitch looked down at Eleanor approvingly.

"An astute observation," Bartimaeus said. He folded his arms. "Your master may have power, Delilah, but you do not. I have over a century of knowledge. The hedgewitch is practically magic incarnate. And if nothing else, Ben can sit on you to keep you from running off for help. So I suggest you run off with your tail between your legs, and find someone with *actual* power to intimidate us with."

Ms. Foster's eyes narrowed. Eleanor could see the calculation running behind her eyes. Finally her brilliant smile returned. "I only wanted to drop by and say hello. I'll be sure to give Mr. January your regards. I'm certain he'll want to speak with you. Soon," she said.

She turned on her heel and strode back out of the house, shoes clicking on the hardwood floors. The sound of the door slamming was followed quickly by an engine starting up.

"She's gone," Ben reported, checking the hall. He shot finger-guns at them. "You were all very impressive."

"That woman just now," Pip said slowly. She was looking out toward the hallway, her eyes not quite focused on anything. "That . . . that was my mom, right?"

"Of course it was," Otto said. "Red hair, killer fashion sense, super evil. She's pretty distinctive." He gave a nervous chuckle.

Pip was frowning. "Right. She was in the January Society, so she was there when they tried to give us to Mr. January?"

"Yes," Eleanor said slowly.

"I think I remember that," Pip said. Her brow furrowed. "Was she nice before? Did I like her?"

Eleanor's mouth fell open. One of the first things she'd ever known about Pip was that she hated her mother, and thought she was evil, even before they figured out it was literally true. Her whole childhood had been shaped by her mother's casual cruelty.

"She was horrible," Otto said, looking stricken. "She was always awful."

"Oh, okay," Pip said. She rubbed the back of her neck. "I guess I can't be that upset that I don't remember her, then."

"That's a pretty big thing to forget," Eleanor said, struggling to keep her voice even. "What else have you forgotten?"

Pip shrugged uncomfortably. "How should I know? I don't remember what I don't remember. I mean, what have *you* forgotten? We've been bouncing around worlds like pinballs, that's got to be doing something to you. World-walker and all."

Eleanor started to reply that she hadn't forgotten anything, and then she stopped. How could she be sure? She'd assumed she would notice when things started to fade, but this wasn't like being Emptied. She might never notice that things were slipping away until she was so far gone she was barely herself anymore. Bright panic welled within her. It was already happening. They were already losing themselves.

She couldn't let it happen. She *couldn't.*

"I don't think I've forgotten anything yet," Otto said. When they looked at him, he dropped his eyes and shuffled his feet. "I checked the mirror. My eyes are totally gray now. And I can just tell. There's all this knowledge, and I can just *want* it and it's mine."

The hedgewitch looked at him with unconcealed envy. "You're young," she said. Her voice was not friendly. "You don't have so very much to lose. You may as well throw yourself into the Story. Get as much from it as you can, before it abandons you."

"No way. I'm not forgetting my family," Otto said fiercely. "Besides, I like learning things the normal way. Knowing things is fine. Finding things out is way more fun."

"So we're all double-doomed now," Pip said with hollow humor.

"We're not doomed," Eleanor said, but it was getting harder and harder to feel it. "The Library. We have to go to the Library."

"We don't have time," Pip said.

Eleanor glared at her. "You're right. We don't. Because if you've already forgotten your *mom,* time is almost up. Getting rid of the Stories doesn't mean getting our memories back. If we don't stop them, there won't be any *us* to save from Mr. January," Eleanor said.

"You and Otto still have plenty of time," Pip said. "The warrior is useful. Way more useful than plain old Pip. Let me help save everyone from Mr. January, and then we can get rid of the Stories. It'll be fine."

If Eleanor hadn't known Pip so well, she might have believed her casual tone and the way she shrugged one shoulder to show she meant every word. But Eleanor saw the way her chin trembled, just a bit. The way her fingers curled when she crossed her arms, to hide the fact that she'd bitten her nails down to nothing.

"We don't know how to fix time. We don't know how to beat Mr. January. But we know how to stop the Stories. It's the one thing we can do, and I'm not going to sit around waiting for my best friends to vanish," Eleanor said.

Pip looked at Otto. "Come on. Back me up here," she said.

But Otto looked at her gravely. "You forgot your mom. What if you forget your dad?" he asked. "What if I forget my sisters and my parents? Eleanor's right. We're not going to win by being heroes. We're going to win by being *us*."

Pip's shoulders slumped. "I don't want to forget my dad. I don't want to forget any of you," she said. "But I'm scared that . . . that just *Pip* won't be enough."

"But it's not just Pip," Ben said, his voice warm. He put a hand on Pip's shoulder. "It's Pip and Eleanor and Otto, the three coolest kids I know. And it's me and Claire—er, whoever you are—and Barry, too."

Slowly, Pip nodded. "Okay. We go to the Library. We destroy the Stories," she said heavily.

"And we fix time," Otto said.

"And *then* we beat Mr. January," Eleanor finished.

"It's not much of a plan," Pip said.

"We've had worse," Eleanor told her. Pip laughed quietly. And then she looked Eleanor in the eye and took a deep breath.

"Let's do this."

Sixteen

They decided to leave immediately. There was no sense in waiting around for Mr. January to show up and stop them, after all.

"I'll get Thea," Eleanor said.

"We're bringing her?" Otto asked.

Eleanor nodded. "I don't want to leave her here when Mr. January is skulking around."

"I'm coming as well," the hedgewitch said. Eleanor gave her a surprised look, and she arched an eyebrow. "I'm not going to pass up visiting the greatest treasury of knowledge in all the worlds."

"Knowledge. That's all you care about, isn't it?" Eleanor asked. "You're not coming along to help us. Just to satisfy your own curiosity."

The hedgewitch was silent for a moment. "Claire thought that I would hurt you, to stop Mr. January. So she fought the

Story tooth and nail, and when it started to take her over, she ran. She was alone and angry when she became the hedgewitch, and that's what the Story devoured, and that's what I became. The only thing I have had for comfort is knowledge, and that is gone, too. I'm trying to learn how to be something more, but it isn't easy, Eleanor."

Eleanor's own anger rose in her. Was she supposed to feel sorry for the hedgewitch? For the person who had destroyed her mother? Her hands balled into fists. She wanted to scream—she wanted to hit the woman—she wanted to run.

Instead, her ears ringing, she marched out of the room and walked up the stairs. She meant to go wake Thea, but at the top of the stairs she stopped and sagged against the wall. She squeezed her eyes shut, choking back a sob.

It hurt so much she couldn't breathe. It hurt so much she could feel the hurt turning swiftly into hate.

The words of *The Glass-Heart Girl* echoed in her mind.

> *"Grief is the consequence of love," said the old woman. "Love will always shatter you, sooner or later. Love is never safe. It is never wise."*
>
> *"But isn't it worth it?" the princess asked.*
>
> *"Worth it to shatter? You can be happy, be whole, by yourself," the old woman chided. "Do not tie yourself strongly to others. Those bonds will tug at you. Pull you apart. You have to stay whole."*

The cold gray thread that bound Eleanor to the hedgewitch was lodged somewhere inside of her, and Eleanor did seem to feel it tugging at her like a fishhook. And it wasn't the only one. Worry about Ben, fear of losing Pip and Otto—they all twisted and tangled and tore at her. If she could cut through them all, she'd be free. She'd have none of this pain.

But she hadn't been able to open the Wending without them. The book was wrong. It had to be. Love had to be worth it, even if it hurt like this.

She straightened up, swiping tears from her eyes, and walked the rest of the way to Thea's room. At the door she paused, looking behind her at the grandfather clock that stood in the hall. The hands weren't moving backward anymore, like usual. They weren't going forward, either. The second hand was ticking forward and back, forward and back, like it was stuck.

Eleanor pushed open the door. Thea sat on the bed. Her arms were wrapped tightly around the cat-of-ashes, who lay draped awkwardly over her shoulder as the girl wept into her long fur.

"Thea?" Eleanor said. "Are you okay?"

Thea looked up, her face streaked with tears and more than a little snot, a great deal of which had smeared into the cat-of-ashes' normally pristine fur.

"Hello, Eleanor," Thea said. She loosened her grip on the cat, who detached herself with what grace she could muster, leaped down from the bed, and walked primly past Eleanor.

"We will never speak of this again," she said under her breath, her tail lashing, and bounded into the hall.

Eleanor sat next to Thea on the bed. Thea stared out the window. Eleanor followed her gaze, but there were only the trees, and the gray beyond them.

"It's like the gray world," Eleanor said. "Last Halloween, we went through Mr. January's door and we ended up in a world like that—all gray mist and gray trees."

"It's an Empty world," Thea said. Eleanor frowned at her, puzzled. "Mother and Father told us about them. You can Empty a world just like you Empty a person. Take everything out—but leave just a little bit. Enough that the world doesn't collapse, because then it would just be destroyed. But if it's that Empty, you can turn it into anything you want."

Like a place to hide twelve magical keys while you hunt for the thirteenth, Eleanor thought. Or a place to hide yourself. That was where the People Who Look Away had been lurking and collecting their keys, so they could get back to the Pallid Kingdom. A gray world—one that they had drained. Eleanor shuddered.

"That's what they're going to do to your world," Thea said. "I mean, what *we're* going to do. We did all those horrible things. To you. To the kids before you."

"You haven't yet," Eleanor said, stroking her hair. "And you don't have to. We don't get to choose what happens to us, Thea, but we all get to choose who we become. Now let's get out of here. The next world will be a better one, I promise."

Thea only curled tighter in on herself. "I miss my brother and sister," she whispered. "Even if they . . ."

"I understand," Eleanor said. "I spent a long time thinking that my mom had tried to hurt me. Or at least didn't try to save me. It's not quite the same thing, but I remember how it felt. I was so, so angry. And I still loved her so much."

"I wish I didn't. I wish I just hated them. It would feel better than this," Thea said. Her chin trembled. "I thought they loved me."

Eleanor put out her hand. Thea drew in a deep, shuddering breath and took Eleanor's hand. In the moment that her fingers touched Eleanor's, the bright thread connecting them glowed stronger, pulsing almost like a heartbeat—and Eleanor had the sudden image of that bright thread going dim.

If she failed, if she lost Thea to her fate, it would break her heart. Even thinking about it hurt.

Maybe *The Glass-Heart Girl* was right. It was easier not to feel, not to fear.

Maybe it was easier to be empty.

Seventeen

When Eleanor got downstairs with Thea in tow, the others were already in the Great Room with Bartimaeus, gathering up their things to leave.

"Thea, are you okay to go now?" Eleanor asked. The girl hadn't said anything, just stared down at her shoes. She nodded without looking up. "Everyone else?"

"Let's get this over with," Pip said.

"Barry and I will hold down the fort," Ben said.

"Can you check in on my family?" Otto asked.

"We'll keep an eye out for them. Don't worry," Ben pledged. He put his hands on Eleanor's shoulders, stooping down to look her in the eye. "Eleanor. Be careful, okay? I need you to come back. I need you to bring Jenny and Naomi back. I need my girls." His voice cracked.

"I will," Eleanor promised him. She wrapped her arms around him. He felt different from the last time she'd seen him—less substantial, less soft—but his hugs were still the very best.

"I'm hitching a ride, too," the cat-of-ashes declared. Eleanor looked at her in surprise. She yawned. "Someone's got to make sure you humans don't cause any more time paradoxes with all your blundering around. If anyone asks, I'm spying on you."

Eleanor snorted. "Fine. The more the merrier."

The kitten-of-ashes hissed from her spot in the hedgewitch's bag. "Have some respect for your elders, puffball," the cat-of-ashes snapped, and the kitten flattened her ears back and hunkered down.

"Be safe, kiddo," Ben said. He reached out and ruffled Eleanor's hair, and then he gave her a friendly little push, like he was sending her on her way.

Eleanor took a steadying breath. And then, blinking away tears, she turned and reached for the Wending.

Library, library, library, she thought, trying to fill her mind with that one, singular thought. But others snuck in. *Mom—the Stories—time's broken—Thea—*

THE LIBRARY OF ENDERSEA, she thought firmly, and the road rippled out from her fingertips, unfurling through the Great Room.

The road was paved with white stone, and to either side of it was white sand, gleaming in the sunlight as a sapphire-blue sea lapped at its shores. The path led up toward towering white cliffs, where seabirds wheeled and called to each other in an excited gabble. At least it looked more pleasant than the Pallid Kingdom.

"Here we go again," Pip muttered. She took Thea's hand and walked past Eleanor. Otto and the hedgewitch followed, the kitten-of-ashes still safely stowed in the hedgewitch's bag. Eleanor cast one last glance back at Ben and Bartimaeus. Ben raised his hand in a wave and cracked a smile that looked out of practice.

"See you soon," Eleanor pledged, and started to step onto the road.

Her heels had barely crossed the barrier between one world and the next when Ben and Bartimaeus began to fade from sight.

In seconds, Eden Eld was gone. There was only the blue sky and the white sand. And a single building, crouched against the pale stone of the cliffs.

"Is that . . . the Library of Endersea?" Pip asked.

"That can't be it," Otto said. "It's tiny."

"It's distinctly unimpressive," the hedgewitch agreed, giving it a skeptical look.

"It's the only building I can see," Eleanor pointed out. "And it is right by the ocean. End of the sea, and all of that."

"I guess we'd better check it out," Pip said with a shrug.

Eleanor had thought the building might be more impressive up close, but as they approached it turned out to be the opposite. The closer they got, the more unassuming the building seemed. It was blocky and dull, with a flat roof and small, dirty windows. Behind them, the waves lapped against the sparkling shore. In front of them, paint flaked off the door and drifted slowly to the ground.

"That *can't* be it," Otto said, but Eleanor pointed. A sign stood in front of the building, weathered from the sand and wind and sea spray.

It read ENDERSEA MUNICIPAL LIBRARY.

Eleanor looked back at the others and spread her hands in a what-can-you-do gesture.

"I was expecting a cathedral of knowledge. This is . . . not that," the hedgewitch noted as they stood on the walk outside the door. There was a book return slot on the side of the building, and flyers in the front windows advertising a summer reading program (the prize was listed as *A TRUTH WHICH HUMAN MINDS CANNOT COMPREHEND* and a $25 gift card to Applebee's).

"Do we go in?" Pip asked.

"We go in," Eleanor said firmly.

She pushed through the door and was immediately greeted by a blast of cool air that smelled intensely and unmistakably like *books*. It took a moment for her eyes to adjust, but when they did, she couldn't quite understand what she was seeing. The outside of the building had been small, but the inside was enormous. They stood on a marble floor in a room paneled with rich oak. Benches lined the edges of the room, and across the lobby was a huge desk, piled with cloth- and leather-bound books.

Pip gave an impressed whistle that echoed off the vaulted ceiling.

"This is more like it," the hedgewitch said approvingly.

Eleanor couldn't disagree. This definitely felt more like a place that would have magical books and endless stores of secret knowledge. She made her way up to the desk. It was as tall as she was, and she had to stretch up on the tips of her toes to reach the bell resting at the edge, a tiny plaque in front of it reading PLEASE RING FOR ASSISTANCE.

The bell made a pleasant little chime that took a while to fade. Eleanor stepped back, and back again, so that she could see over the desk to the doors on the wall behind it.

"Do you think we should wait, or just go in?" Otto said, but before Eleanor could answer, the doors swung open and someone—or something—stepped through.

The being striding through the doors had to be at least ten feet tall. He was towering and spindly looking, with a vaguely human-shaped body—at least, as far as she could tell with it being under long blue robes—but a head that looked distinctly goatlike. He was carrying a number of books in his two right arms, while a third arm on the left gripped a clipboard. A small, battered plastic name tag pinned to his robes read THE LIBRARIAN, and below that, HE/HIM. He peered over half-moon spectacles at them.

"Yes?" he said.

"Are you the librarian?" Eleanor asked. What she'd immediately thought to ask was *Are you going to eat us?* but that didn't seem polite.

"No, I am the Librarian," the creature said.

"Isn't that what I said?" Eleanor stammered.

"It's capitalized. You didn't capitalize it," the Librarian said, blinking at her. Eleanor wasn't sure how he could tell whether she'd capitalized it, since she'd been speaking out loud, but she decided not to argue.

"I'm sorry. The Librarian, then," she said, and he gave an approving nod. "We're looking for the Prime Stories."

He raised an eyebrow. "Which ones?"

Eleanor frowned. "All three of them?"

"Three? You think there are *three*?" the Librarian said with a warm chuckle. "Young lady, the Library contains the largest collection of predatory Stories in all the worlds. Here, let me get a better look at you." He came around the side of the desk. A fourth hand appeared from under his robes, and he raised it to adjust his glasses. "Ah. You are the Gray Tales, if I'm not mistaken. Warrior, witch, and world-walker." He pointed at each of them in turn.

"That's right. And we'd like to see them. Us. The original Stories, or whatever," Eleanor asked, trying to sound confident and trailing off helplessly. "They're, like, actual books, right?"

"Like actual books, yes," the Librarian repeated, as if speaking to a particularly dim-witted potato.

Eleanor gave the Librarian a bright smile. "Yes. We'd like to see our Stories, please."

"But of course," the Librarian said with a flourish of one hand—Eleanor thought it might have been the one that had been holding the clipboard a moment ago, but it might have been a new one altogether. Then, suddenly, the Librarian froze.

"Is that," he said, enunciating each word with painful precision, "a cat?"

"Yes?" Eleanor said, looking over at the cat-of-ashes, who was sitting well off to the side, grooming herself with apparent disinterest.

The Librarian drew himself up. "We do not allow pets in the library."

The cat-of-ashes stiffened. "I am no pet," she said in a low, dangerous purr.

"Mew," the kitten-of-ashes agreed, equally affronted.

The Librarian sniffed. "Nonetheless, *cats* are not permitted. Many of the books are allergic. The rest of you may follow me. I will show you to the proper section." He beckoned them with long, many-jointed fingers.

"Are you okay staying out here?" Eleanor asked the cat-of-ashes.

The cat-of-ashes lashed her tail. "Fine."

"You'll have to—"

"I'll watch the puffball," the cat-of-ashes snapped. The hedgewitch set the kitten-of-ashes down, and the kitten immediately skittered across the marble floor to attack her older self's tail. "Don't take too long," the cat-of-ashes said resignedly, pinning the kitten to the floor with one massive paw.

"Thea, do you want to stay with the cats?" Eleanor asked, but Thea shook her head mutely. "Stick close," Eleanor told her, and hurried to follow the Librarian.

Beyond the doors, a dizzying landscape of books spilled out in every direction. The group had stepped out onto a landing.

To either side stairways swooped up and down, leading to more and more levels. The library was circular, with shelves spiraling inward. From their vantage point, Eleanor could see only the beginning of the spiral and the hallways that led toward the center, but somehow she could sense the way it wound inward. The center, she was certain, held something important.

The center was where they needed to go.

But the Librarian instead led them along the edge of the spiral, staying against the outer wall of the library. At regular intervals, hallways led farther outward into rooms labeled PROPHECIES—FALSE, and PROMISES—BROKEN.

"You said there were other Stories," Eleanor said as she trotted to keep up with the Librarian's long strides. The hedgewitch, holding Thea's hand, lagged behind. "What other Stories? We thought it was just the three of us. How many more are there?"

"See for yourself," the Librarian said. He had stopped in front of an archway, above which read in golden letters STORIES—PERSONIFIED, MANIFEST, AND INFECTIOUS.

Beyond the archway was a room the size of the Great Room at Ashford House. In the center of the room was a long wooden table, several chairs set beside it. Every wall was covered in shelves from floor to ceiling, and every shelf was filled with books—thick ones and slender ones, leather books and three-ring binders, loose papers bound with twine.

"These are all Stories?" Eleanor asked in wonder, turning slowly. "Like ours?"

"Each volume represents a Story, yes, but their similarities to yours vary wildly," the Librarian said. "Is it such a surprise? Everyone tells Stories. Some of these came into being only once and ended. Others, like yours, are more persistent, recurring. The Gray collection should be . . . ah, here we are. A three-volume set."

He crossed the room in two enormous strides. Two arms appeared from under his robe—one on the left, one on the right. With one he extracted three thick tomes from the shelf, stacking them in the crook of his other arm. Eleanor counted his arms—there were six, now.

"How many arms do you think he *has*?" Otto asked under his breath.

"Always one fewer than I need," the Librarian replied dryly. He set the books on the table in a line, then tapped each cover with one long finger. "Warrior. Witch. World-walker. You are free to peruse them, but you must leave by closing."

"When is that?" Eleanor asked politely.

"The end of time, and not a moment later," the goatish creature said sternly. "Also"—here he pinned Thea with his gaze—"no touching the books if your hands are *sticky*. Now, I will leave you to it. If you need me, you need only say the words 'assistance, please.'"

He gave them a polite nod and departed, gliding out at a serene but rapid pace.

"What a remarkable creature," the hedgewitch mused. She extracted her hand from Thea's and drifted toward the shelves, eyeing the other Stories with interest.

"So what do we do?" Pip asked. "Burn them? Tear the pages out?"

"We're not supposed to damage library books," Otto reminded her. She gave him a withering look.

Eleanor held up a placating hand. "We should take a look at them first. Besides, I'm guessing we're going to have to get out of here fast after we do destroy them, and we want to look for information to help us fix time and beat Mr. January, too, right?"

The three of them, Thea in tow, approached the table where the Librarian had left the books. They were massive, as thick as Eleanor's hand was long. Instead of a usual binding, they had metal hinges, and latches to hold them shut. There were no titles on the covers, just symbols. The one on the left showed a flower with vines curling around it. The second, a sword that was instantly recognizable as the one at Pip's hip: Gloaming. And the third had a pattern of lines that might have been branching roads.

Eleanor moved to the end of the line, undoing the latch on her own Story, and hauled the book open to a page in the middle.

The text looked handwritten, elegant letters flowing over the page, interspersed with a few small illustrations. It described the travels of a young man it called "the weaver of roads." Eleanor flipped through a few pages, skimming the tale as the young man visited strange worlds and kingdoms. Then the letters began to fade, until by the end of the next page they had vanished completely—and a new story faded in, this one about an old woman setting out from her home after her husband died, wanting to see the world.

"It's everyone who's ever been the world-walker. All of their stories," Eleanor marveled, reading snippets out loud to the others.

"This one, too," Otto confirmed. "Wow. There have been a *lot* of hedgewitches."

"I bet you a hundred bucks there are way more Jacks than that," Pip said. "Yours mostly fade out. Look at this." She flipped through, showing page after page that cut off abruptly—usually when the current Jack was eaten by a dragon or crushed by an avalanche.

Otto ran his fingers along the pages with a frown on his face. "I don't think these are the real Stories," he said.

"What do you mean?" Eleanor asked, alarmed.

"They don't *feel* magical. And look. Inside the back cover." He flipped to the end.

Tacked inside the back cover of the book was a little label. ARCHIVAL REPRODUCTION. In even smaller text below it read THE LIBRARY ASSUMES NO LEGAL, MORAL, OR MAGICAL RESPONSIBILITY FOR THE CONSEQUENCES OF IMPROPER READING, COPYING, OR REVIEWING OF DANGEROUS TEXTS.

"These are all just copies," Otto said in frustration, gesturing around at the walls.

The hedgewitch, who had been idly flipping through a slim volume titled *The Skin Thieves*, made a humming sound in the back of her throat. "I think that might be for the best. These things obviously need proper handling. Too dangerous for the public."

"What's in that one?" Otto asked curiously, but she shuddered and snapped it shut.

"You may be the hedgewitch now, Otto, but you're still only thirteen. You do not need to see what's in that book," she said firmly, putting it back on the shelf.

"So what are we supposed to do?" Pip asked, throwing her hands into the air. "Destroying the *copies* won't do anything."

"I guess we can ask for the originals," Eleanor suggested. "What were we supposed to say?"

"Assistance, please," said Thea helpfully, and a split second later the Librarian was there, gliding through the door. He'd set down the books he had been carrying the last time they saw him and had all his arms hidden under his robes.

"How may I assist you?" he asked.

"Ah. Well, thank you very much for showing us these books," Eleanor said. "But they aren't *quite* what we're looking for."

"No?" he said. "They are the records of your Stories. I am certain of that."

"We need the originals. The *actual* Stories," Eleanor said.

The Librarian frowned faintly, one furry ear flicking. "The original manuscripts are not available to the public," he said.

"But we're not just the public. They're *our* Stories." Pip sounded affronted. Eleanor had once found a library book in

Pip's room that was three years overdue because she hadn't gotten around to reading it yet. Pip was not the ideal library patron.

"Your Stories are *living* Stories. That means that they are still in the process of being written," the Librarian said. "It makes them extremely volatile. Only experts can handle such temperamental books, much less make the necessary updates."

"What experts? Can we talk to them?" Otto asked.

The Librarian's nostrils flared. Now he was definitely getting annoyed. "Absolutely not. The Editor's work is delicate, and she does not like to be interrupted."

"We couldn't even take a look?" Pip pressed.

"No, you may not. The Editor is not to be disturbed under any circumstances. Now if that is all—"

"Yes, of course. We're very sorry for bothering you," Eleanor said quickly. "We'll let you know if we need anything else."

"The youths these days," the Librarian said to himself, and wafted out of the room with an air of deep aggrievement.

"I guess we have to find the Editor," Pip said.

"I think I know where she is," Eleanor replied. She crooked a finger to indicate the others should follow her, and walked out of the side room, back to the landing that wrapped around the outside of the library. She pointed across the way, to the huge spiral of shelves.

"What we need is in there," she said. "Right in the center." It sang to her, a humming along the threads of the world. There was something there. A secret way. The world-walker knew the way to secret things, and so Eleanor knew as well, as vividly as she knew her own name.

Except that wasn't exactly true.

Because for one terrifying moment, as Eleanor looked toward the spiral and saw, somehow, the whole interior of it, all the pieces that were hidden from her eyes, she knew the spiral far better than she knew her own name.

For one moment, hardly the space of a heartbeat, she didn't know her name at all.

Eighteen

"Keep an eye out for the Librarian," Eleanor instructed Pip as they hurried across the walkway that connected the outer ring of the library to the inner spiral.

"Technically we're not doing anything wrong," Otto said. "He didn't say to stay out of the spiral."

"We're not doing anything wrong *yet*," Pip said, a little gleam in her eye.

"Are we going to get in trouble?" Thea asked. She held the hedgewitch's hand once again. The hedgewitch did not seem thrilled about this but hadn't pulled away.

"It'll be okay," Eleanor assured her. "Right now we're just exploring." Somewhere inside the spiral were the real Stories. Before they could figure out how to get them, they had to *find* them. The spiral wound and wound, the walls curling gradually tighter around them.

Categories were printed in tiny gold letters on the shelves. They passed LIES—COMFORTING and LEFT-HANDED AUTHORS and HAS A DOG IN IT. Otto read each one as they passed—out loud, until Pip shushed him.

And then, quite suddenly, they had reached the center of the spiral. The walls of shelves drew together and then ended at a thin, empty wall, about as wide as Eleanor's shoulders.

"This seems to be the end of the road," the hedgewitch said with a note of doubt in her voice. Eleanor frowned. There should have been something here.

NOVELS WITH SONGS IN THEM, the final section on the left read. On the right was DISAPPOINTING ENDINGS. Neither one seemed particularly forbidden, and neither contained the Stories they were looking for.

"It's a dead end," Pip said, frustrated.

"Hold on," Eleanor said. That little sense inside her was insisting that she keep going. She followed that tug, that glimmer, drawing closer to the blank wall at the end of the spiral.

There was a tiny golden sign affixed to the center of the wall, a little bit above her head. It read AUTHORIZED PERSONNEL ONLY.

"A hidden door?" Otto suggested.

"Maybe," Eleanor said. She reached out her hand and put her palm against the wall. There was nothing on the other side; she was certain of it. But there was something *strange* about this spot.

She could sense the way forward, but something was blocking her. She was not authorized personnel.

"But I am the world-walker," she muttered. All ways were open to her. She shut her eyes and focused. *Let me through.*

There was one last hitch of resistance, and then—

"Are you going to do anything?" Pip asked, impatient. She was shifting from foot to foot, clearly eager to get moving again.

"I thought I did," Eleanor said. But they were still standing in the same spot, with the same shelves looming around them.

Except they weren't the same shelves. They weren't the same books. The categories had changed. One looming shelf contained a half-dozen categories of CURSES, ranked by severity. On the other side were FAILED SAINTS. The books had an odd kind of shivering, humming presence to them. As if they were alive. As if they were *breathing.*

Even the sign on the wall had changed. Instead of AUTHORIZED PERSONNEL ONLY, it now read PUBLIC COLLECTION, with a little arrow to point forward.

"We aren't in the same spiral," Otto said in wonder.

"And I don't think we're supposed to be here, so we should hurry," Eleanor said.

"Where do we go?" Otto asked.

"There's only one way *to* go," Pip pointed out, nodding back the way they had come. They traipsed off again, though with a touch more caution this time. The books seemed to watch them as they went, rustling among themselves. Eleanor kept close to Pip, and to Gloaming. The hedgewitch studied the titles of the books.

"I wouldn't touch these," she said, after leaning in close to examine a fat black tome with red ribbons dangling from it. "They don't seem well contained."

"I wasn't planning on it," Eleanor said, but as she glanced back toward the hedgewitch she glimpsed Thea. The girl had fallen behind and was staring at the shelves in front of her. Eleanor hurried back toward her.

"Thea, don't touch them," she said.

Thea gave a little jump and looked up guiltily. "They're ours, though," she said.

Eleanor frowned, coming up to stand at Thea's shoulder. Four books stood in a row. Two of them were the color of bone, two a pale gray. On the shelf below them was a tidy golden label: THE ROYAL FAMILY OF THE PALLID KINGDOM.

"That's us," Thea said. "Why are there books about us? And why are there only four? There should be five, shouldn't there?"

"I don't know," Eleanor said, feeling uneasy. "But I think we should leave them where they are." She held out her hand. Reluctantly, Thea took it, and Eleanor drew her away, casting one last glance over her shoulder. The books were a pale splotch on the shelf, standing alone from the rest. As if the other books didn't appreciate their company.

They walked for several more minutes before they reached the end of the spiral. Beyond was a cavernous vault and an almost unbroken expanse of white marble floor.

In the middle of that empty space was a drafting table, and behind it sat a creature that looked identical to the Librarian, except for the bright red of their robe. All around them were piled massive stacks of books. Some were leaning, others had already toppled, sliding and merging into book hills and book mountains. The creature held a red pen in one long-fingered hand, scribbling in the book on their desk; with another hand they turned the pages back and forth. Eleanor could hear the faint *scratch-scratch-scratch* of the pen from all the way near the spiral.

Their footsteps were louder without the books to muffle them. Eleanor's shoes squeaked on the marble tile, and Pip clomped along beside her. *Squeak-clomp-squeak-clomp.* Eleanor winced.

It was an excruciatingly long walk to the Editor's desk, their shoes making a racket all the way. As they grew closer the Editor grew larger, until they stood in front of the desk, the edge of which was well above Eleanor's head. This close, Eleanor could make out the writing on the Editor's name tag—THE EDITOR, SHE/HER, it read.

"Ah. Mm. Interesting," the Editor murmured. "'And walked up to the Editor's table, interrupting her work.' Humph." She looked over the edge of the drafting table at last, peering down at Eleanor and the others. "Most unusual. I am not accustomed to appearing in the pages of my own books, Eleanor."

"How do you know my name?" Eleanor asked in surprise.

The Editor extended a third hand to pick up one of the books she had been working on and hold it out so that Eleanor could read the spine.

Eleanor Barton, it said.

She sucked in a sharp breath. "You have *my* book?" she asked.

"Hm. Yes. But we would have saved a few words if you didn't ask questions to which the answers are obvious," the Editor said. "Concision, Eleanor. It's an important skill."

"Does everyone have a book here?" Otto asked with interest.

"A better question," the Editor said, nodding approvingly. Her hands continued to move across the pages of the two books, the end of the quill dipping and flicking. "No. Only certain people. And it's not something to aspire to. Being turned into a tale that can be contained in a book makes you rather vulnerable."

"Vulnerable to what?" Eleanor asked.

"To being changed. Deliberate sabotage. Transcription errors. Water damage," the Editor said. "People are a big messy beautiful bunch of stories. It takes a great deal of effort to alter them. A book, though, that's easy. Now. You are here to steal the Stories to which you are bound, correct?"

Eleanor started to lie, but then she stopped. Could she even lie to someone who was literally writing her story?

"I'm not writing it. Merely editing it. Oh, go on, then. Take a look," the Editor said. She offered Eleanor her own book again, and this time Eleanor took it. Her skin tingled when she touched it.

Tentatively, she opened the front cover. The title page read *Eleanor Barton*, but below it in red ink had been added *the World-Walker*. Eleanor flipped forward.

Eleanor Barton was born cursed, the first sentence read.

This was her life. This was her story. She skimmed the pages, flipping forward through her childhood—and then stopped. Only a few pages in, the steady parade of black ink stopped, interrupted by a paragraph written in scarlet.

Eleanor had always had a knack for finding hidden things—secret doors and shortcuts. She never truly lost her way, for even when she did not arrive where she meant to, she found that she was where she ought *to be.*

It felt true. She remembered that about herself. But she was suddenly quite sure she shouldn't. "You're writing the Story over me," Eleanor said, her voice a dry croak.

"It is an extensive revision," the Editor acknowledged.

"What did this used to say?" Eleanor demanded.

The Editor considered. "I *believe* it was something about your best friend in third grade. Ellery. You liked that your names started the same way. You thought that you sounded like the characters in the kind of book where two friends found a magical world behind a garden wall."

Eleanor looked past the Editor at the stack of books beside the worktable. Some of the titles she didn't recognize, but there, in a neat pile, were ones she knew very well. *Otto Ellis. Philippa Foster.*

"You're rewriting all of us," Eleanor said. She felt a bit sick.

"Yes, and at an increasingly rapid pace. You're not my only books, you know. But you are taking up an absurd amount of my time. And you're not content with only your own books, no! Look at this! Do you have any idea how many of these are here because of you?" She waved her hand at the stacks of books beside her. She plucked one from the stack and brandished it at them. Eleanor sucked in a breath as she saw the title on the cover.

The Small, Cursed Town of Eden Eld.

The Editor slammed it down onto the desk. "I am the only Editor in this place, and we have stories from every world. *Every. World.* Which is why I really cannot afford to be interrupted. If you had any idea the stress I'm under, you would understand." She revealed two more hands, just so she could bury her face in them and groan.

"She sounds like my dad when he's on deadline," Pip muttered. The hedgewitch snorted in amusement.

Eleanor was still staring. "You have a book for Eden Eld?"

The Editor reached over and flipped through it. The pages were splattered with random globs and lines of red ink. "It's a travesty. Absolute chaos," she said. A page detached from the binding and slipped onto the table.

"Can you fix it?" Otto asked.

She made a hum of mixed annoyance and agreement. "Luckily, most of the other continuity errors have mostly sorted themselves out. Minor holes, nothing world-breaking," the Editor said. "This book is the only one that's truly a mess. The only way to fix it would be to correct the original paradox by returning the girl to her timeline . . ."

"Not happening," Eleanor, Pip, and Otto said together.

". . . or reverting to the previous draft," the Editor said. "We always make a backup anytime there are major changes like this. I can use it to return the text to its state right before the timeline changed. In this case, the moment of the eclipse."

"Everyone would come back?" Eleanor asked. "And the January Society, they'd be gone?"

"Indeed."

"And Thea—she'll still be Thea?" Eleanor asked.

The Editor nodded. "It creates some contradictions, of course. Katie Rhodes existed, but doesn't anymore. Thea shouldn't exist, but does. But it should all hold together well enough to prevent any further damage."

"Great," Pip said. "Let's do that, then. And then we can go back and have plenty of time to deal with Mr. January."

Eleanor let out a sigh of relief. That was *one* problem sorted, at least. "Then we just need the Prime Stories," she said.

The Editor pursed her lips. "I really can't give them to you. They're part of the restricted collection. The books here are very dangerous, Eleanor. They can take a person over completely. Write themselves onto your soul. Blot you out completely."

The hedgewitch had taken a book from the Editor's desk and was flipping through it with an intent look of interest. "Fascinating," she muttered. She was so absorbed in the book that she wasn't watching Thea anymore. Eleanor hadn't been, either. None of them had been.

None of them, Eleanor suddenly realized, had noticed that she was creeping closer and closer to the stacks of books. Or that she had stood on her tiptoes to reach up, grabbing hold of the very edge of a particularly thick book.

Or that she had pulled it down into her arms and opened the cover.

Nineteen

The book Thea was clutching was pale gray, with the faintest hints of violet. And on its cover was written *Princess Thea of the Pallid Kingdom*.

"Don't touch that!" the Editor cried. "It hasn't been updated yet! It could—"

Her voice cut off with a strangled sound, but Eleanor didn't have to ask what it could do. It was already happening.

Words were crawling up Thea's arms, scuttling beneath her sleeves. They snaked up her throat and flowed up to her eyes, until it seemed like she was weeping words.

"Thea!" Eleanor shouted. She and Pip grabbed the book, trying to pry it from Thea's hands. Eleanor wrapped a hand around Thea's wrist like she could stop the words from flowing into her.

But both of them were too late. The last of the words had slithered free of the pages, settling into Thea's skin. She let go of the book and staggered back. Her eyes were black, swimming with ink. Her outline blurred.

"I never escaped," Thea said. Her voice held an odd echo, as if it was coming from far away. She stumbled back one step, and then another. "None of us escaped. We stayed and grew up and we learned to be hard and cold."

A girl, another Thea, stepped free of her. This one was older. Her hair had lost its color, turning platinum. "We learned not to show our true faces. We learned to lie and to bargain and to gather power and to keep it."

Her outline shivered again, and Katie Rhodes stepped free, the way she'd looked as she hunted them down the road. "We went into the world to conquer it, but the gates were sealed shut behind us. And so we waited. And we schemed. And we were wicked."

Their heads tilted as one. "You tried to save me," the youngest Thea whispered. "But you failed."

The two Theas stepped back—and vanished. Only Katie Rhodes remained. She rolled her shoulders and then her neck, as if working out the kinks. "Come, Shatterblack. Come, Rag-a-bone. Your mistress is back. It's time to stop hiding." She lifted her hands, a smile stretching across her beautiful face, and the marble floor split open like overripe fruit, the road rushing through it.

Shatterblack leaped, an arc of black. Rag-a-bone darted, pale fur blending with the white marble floor. Pip had Gloaming out in less than a second, and caught Shatterblack with the flat of it, taking the hound's weight and then tossing her away. The Editor ducked behind her desk, holding a thick tome over her head for protection.

The hedgewitch tossed a loop of what looked like simple twine at Rag-a-bone. Brambles grew from the floor, tangling the hound. Otto reached a hand into the hedgewitch's bag and pulled out a slim book. He opened it like he knew exactly what he was looking for, held out a hand, and shouted a single syllable. There was a *pop* and a flash of light right in front of Shatterblack's nose, making her shriek and veer away just as she jumped for Pip again.

Katie stood seething, her hair as white as the hounds' blazing eyes.

"You made me think that I could be different. You made me think that you would protect me," Katie hissed. Her words were like a whisper right in Eleanor's ear.

"You don't have to be her. You can be Thea," Eleanor said pleadingly.

But Katie shook her head. "I would have broken if I stayed Thea. I had to become something else, to stay whole," she said.

"What nonsense is this?!" the Librarian roared, striding out from the spiral. "This area is restricted! None of you should be here! And now there are dogs? *In the Library?*" He crossed the distance in a few steps. Rag-a-bone and Shatterblack snarled and jumped for him. Two hands darted out from under his robes and caught them by the scruff, holding them aloft and giving them a good shake. More hands shot out, catching Otto and Pip and Eleanor by the arms. The hedgewitch tried to dodge away, but he got her, too, holding them all in an uncomfortable cluster to one side, while the hounds growled and twisted on the other.

"Your borrowing privileges are hereby revoked!" the Librarian said sternly.

"I do apologize." Katie stepped forward, her gray skirt trailing, a faint, polite smile on her lips. "I am afraid this is all my fault," she said. "I came to take these miscreants home. I didn't mean to disrupt your incredible library. If you hand them over to me, I will make sure they do not trouble you again."

"Humph," the Librarian said, considering.

"Don't listen to her!" Otto said. The Librarian gave him a little shake.

"No one is going anywhere until I get an explanation for this nonsense," the Librarian said.

"Ah. In that case . . ." Katie's outline flexed—and suddenly there were three of her. One of them threw up a hand, and the air shimmered with hard light. The Librarian's hand shot out, but it hit the light and rebounded.

The other two Katies wheeled, sprinting for the Editor. One of them veered toward the stack of books. The other grabbed something off the desk itself.

"Stop her!" the Editor yelled in a panic. The Librarian dropped all of them, hounds included, and dived for the third Katie, but he was too late. She was already pelting back toward the road, and so were the other two, the hounds right at their heels. Pip started after them, but Eleanor grabbed her by the elbow, hauling her back.

The three Katies reached the road, melding back into each other. The hounds leaped on after her. The Librarian yelled in goatish fury, but Katie just winked—and the road disappeared.

Twenty

The Library was once again silent. Except for the Editor. "Oh no oh no oh no," she was chanting. "This can't be happening. This can't be happening."

"What is it? What did she get?" Otto asked.

The Librarian, panting, looked down at the Editor's desk in horror. "She took a pot of ink. The *red* ink," he said.

"And one of my quills. And who knows how many books," the Editor said despairingly.

"What happened?" Eleanor asked, still reeling.

The Editor looked regretfully down at her. "I hadn't edited Thea's book yet. The story inside it was still the old one—the one where she didn't escape the Pallid Kingdom as a child. When she touched her own book, it wrote itself inside her."

"The Eden Eld book is gone," the hedgewitch noted. "Katie must have taken it."

Eleanor groaned. She scanned the table, hoping the hedge-witch was wrong. But there was no sign of the book. Hers was still there, at least—and Otto's and Pip's. That was a small relief.

The only relief in a sea of sorrow. Thea was gone. Those words had flowed into her, and every horrible thing that had happened to her and every wicked thing she had done had rushed back in.

"Does that mean time is fixed?" Otto asked hopefully.

"For the most part," the Editor said. "I'll have to revert some of the changes I've been making, but everything should go back to how it used to be on its own. Except . . ."

"Except what?" Pip asked sharply.

The Editor flicked an ear anxiously. "She has Eden Eld's book. Which means she can prevent the paradoxes there from repairing themselves. Override reality."

"Do you have any idea how much damage she could do to those books with that ink?" the Librarian asked.

"What about damage to Eden Eld?" Otto asked. Eleanor felt sick. What was Katie going to do? Would she destroy Eden Eld completely with a flick of the quill?

Thea wouldn't do that, she thought. But Katie wasn't Thea anymore. *Because you couldn't save her.*

"It's not a simple process. She won't be able to do too much all at once," the Editor said, swiveling an ear back. "There may be some time before things go too horribly awry. Of course, they were fairly awry already."

"This is a disaster. No books have been stolen from the Library in all my six hundred years of service," the Librarian moaned, covering his face.

"We'll get them back," Eleanor pledged, though her voice shook. "The books and the ink and the quill."

The Editor and the Librarian looked at each other. "Is that allowed?" the Editor asked.

"Technically speaking, we are responsible for all retrieval efforts," the Librarian said in a hushed whisper, though they could all hear it clearly.

"I'm not cut out for fieldwork. I have tendinitis," the Editor whispered back, leaning her head in close to the Librarian's.

"They *are* heroes," the Librarian allowed. "And it *is* an unprecedented emergency."

"Not to mention board game night. We wouldn't want to skip board game night," the Editor replied.

Together, they turned toward the four humans. The Librarian cleared his throat. "Given the extraordinary circumstances, we will allow you to retrieve our books and supplies."

"And what do we get in return?" Eleanor asked, folding her arms.

The Librarian looked affronted. "A sense of civic duty fulfilled!"

"No way," Otto said, shoulder to shoulder with Eleanor. "We want the Stories."

"The Stories belong to the Library's collection," the Librarian said. He hesitated. "But I suppose we could let you check them out, with a generous return policy."

"What about the damaged books policy?" Pip asked, with a tone of voice that suggested extensive experience with the topic.

The Librarian's eye twitched. But the Editor chuckled. "Come with me," she said, and beckoned them forward.

THEY LEFT THE Librarian to tidy up all the books that had been scattered in the fight. The Editor led them to a tall, narrow door with nine strong locks, which she turned all at once with nine keys held in nine hands. On the other side was a large room lined with shelves. The books on the shelves were locked behind firm iron grates. The Editor crossed to one, muttering to herself, and unlocked it.

"Here we are," she said. She carried three slim volumes to the table in the middle of the room and set them down one by one. "Warrior. Witch. World-walker."

The books hummed. Eleanor could hear them. Feel them. Her mouth felt suddenly dry. Pip made a weird little *unf* noise and rocked on her feet, and Otto's fingers twitched.

Eleanor crept forward. The books called to her. She wanted to lunge for them. She wanted to wrap her arms around that third book with its purple cover and press it against her chest until it sank right into her rib cage. That feeling urged her to surrender, let the Story consume her. Shaking, she held herself back.

"There they are," the hedgewitch said wonderingly. There was something forlorn in her expression. Everything she'd lost was right in the pages of the second book.

"How do we destroy them?" Pip asked.

The Editor looked pained. "They're books. Water, fire, a good pair of scissors—any of them should do the trick." She fidgeted. "But I do wonder if you *want* to destroy them. They're marvelous things. Dangerous, but marvelous."

Eleanor knew what she meant. The world-walker's power was amazing. It would have been more amazing if she wasn't constantly using it while running for her life, but still—she could go anywhere. Visit other *worlds.*

"I've barely gotten to do any magic," Otto said, and sighed. "I wouldn't mind forgetting third grade if I could do a few spells and make some potions."

"Yeah, being the warrior is pretty awesome. Except for the not being me part," Pip admitted. "But we've got to do it. Right?"

"Right," Eleanor said. "We're forgetting too fast. We're losing ourselves." But still she didn't move toward the books. She looked over at the Editor. "Is there any way to keep the good parts, but not lose ourselves?"

The Editor considered. "Not normally. The Story writes itself over you. That's how it works."

Otto frowned. "But Bartimaeus said that the Stories have to have physical copies, because if a wild story just gets inside a person, it changes to be theirs. To be part of them."

Eleanor tapped a finger against her lips. "When we first found out about the Prime Stories, Jack said that the Stories are a curse because stories are *simple.* Something that can fit in a book is straightforward. *People* are complicated. They're made up of lots and lots of stories and versions of themselves, and they can hold all of it. The Stories replace that with one simple version, erasing all the rest. But what if . . ." She trailed off, frowned, a thought starting to form. She looked at the Editor. "Is there a way to take the Stories out of the books? So that they would become *part* of us, like wild stories, instead of *replacing* us?"

"Ah," the Editor said, considering. She cocked her head to the side. "Normally, I would say no. But your abilities, Eleanor, may hold the key. It's possible that you could take the Stories out of their books before putting them inside you. It would spare your memories and personalities but it would mean the Stories wouldn't hold their power for very long. They'd fade into you, over time."

"Assuming it works at all, and you don't just end up erased immediately," the hedgewitch said. "It's a risky proposition."

"But then we could have their power. *Without* losing ourselves," Pip said. "We could use them to fight the People Who Look Away, at least for a while."

"How would we do it?" Eleanor asked.

"The mechanism is similar to the one used to create the Empty," Otto said. They looked at him, startled, and he blinked. "Ooh. Hedgewitch knowledge. Let's see what I know." His face scrunched up like he was concentrating.

"You don't have to make that face," the hedgewitch said, but not very loudly.

"I think . . . I think you should be able to do it, Eleanor. Your abilities can open connections between worlds, but they can connect people, too. You have to make a connection to the Stories, just wide enough to let them in slowly."

"Wait. Does that mean Eleanor could Empty someone, if she wanted to?" Pip asked.

"Of course not," Eleanor said, though something twisted in the pit of her stomach.

"I don't know about this. We came here to destroy the Stories. Maybe we still should. I mean, what if something goes wrong?" Otto asked.

"I could take the Story back from you," the hedgewitch said softly, her eyes fixed on the slim book. "You could put it into me, instead of risking yourself, Otto."

"That would be unwise," the Editor said.

"Why?" the hedgewitch demanded, almost snarling. "Why shouldn't I have it back?"

"Because you have been completely rewritten once already, and you have not had enough time to get complicated again," the Editor said. "You are too fragile. That Story would burn through you in an instant."

The hedgewitch's jaw clenched, and for a moment Eleanor thought she was going to argue. But she only turned on her heel and strode away, her steps ringing on the marble.

That's where I got that habit from, Eleanor thought. She always had to just walk away when she got too angry.

"What if we're wrong? What if they just destroy us?" Pip whispered.

"There's only one way to find out," Eleanor said. She squared her shoulders. She stepped forward. And she picked up the book of the world-walker.

At first, it was like she was drowning. Wind roared in her ears, and with it came the clamor of a hundred voices crying out, shouting words she could barely understand. The words were crashing into her, tearing through her. *I was wrong*, she thought in a panic. It was going to destroy her! It was going to hollow her out, and she'd be as gone as if she were Empty.

Empty.

In the midst of the howling gale, gripping the book tightly in her hands, she thought of how Melia had stolen her feelings from her. How she and Ash had plucked things from people or sneaked them in. She remembered how it had felt—and suddenly, the world-walker filling her mind and her soul, she realized how it was done.

It was all in the connections. She was connected to the Story. She could see the connection—and she could control it.

Stop, she thought, pushing back against the bond that linked her to the ravenous Story. The howling gale quieted. Slowly,

slowly, she drew the Story toward her, letting it seep gently into the gaps and cracks. The shouting turned to whispers.

. . . and wander through starlight, through moonbeams . . .

. . . every road open to her . . .

. . . never lost, for she always found her way, though she did not always know it . . .

Eleanor opened her eyes as the Story flowed gently, steadily into her.

She was gripping the book with both hands. Pip and Otto were babbling, shouting, but the Editor held them back with several of her long arms. Eleanor could see why they were so alarmed.

Words were climbing up her arms. They swirled up toward her sleeves and vanished below, flowing out of the book. *Companions*, she saw, and *the Wending* and *but some roads are dangerous.* And as they flowed into her, she didn't need to read them. She knew them.

She kept her breathing steady, focusing on slowing the Story down, on finding places to tuck it away or weave it into herself.

The last of the words seeped into Eleanor and lay on her skin like wet ink.

"Eleanor?" Otto asked, uncertain.

Eleanor looked at him, but she didn't just see him. The web of shimmering threads was *everywhere* now, and not just in this room. She could sense the threads flowing out through the walls. Beyond the library, even, dazzling and endless.

"I'm okay," she said, smiling. "I'm me." Eleanor Barton. Claire Barton's daughter. Friend to Otto and Pip. She wasn't sure what she might have misplaced in that first rush of words, but all the essential bits of her seemed to be in place.

She was still holding the book, but it didn't hum anymore. She flipped it open. Every page was blank.

"*Fascinating,*" the Editor and Otto said together, and flashed each other reflexive smiles.

"Me next," Otto declared, stepping forward.

"I think I can get it right from the start this time," Eleanor said. She put two fingertips against Otto's temple, and two against the cover of the hedgewitch's Story, and let the words begin to flow.

Twenty-One

It was a slower process with Otto and Pip, but eventually all three Stories were empty—or rather, the books were empty, and the Stories were written on their skin. Otto kept pulling up his shirt and peering at the tiny text, trying to make out every word, but Pip pulled her sleeves down firmly and didn't glance.

The Librarian and Editor showed them out to the lobby, where the cats were waiting. The kitten-of-ashes had fallen asleep curled against the cat-of-ashes, and the older cat was idly grooming the kitten's fur, leaving it sticking straight up behind her head.

"You're short a princess," the cat-of-ashes noted.

"Long story," Otto said. The cat-of-ashes narrowed her eyes but didn't press.

The Librarian folded two of his hands. "Please be prompt in returning with the ink and quill, and the pilfered books. Reality itself may be counting on you," he said. Four more hands emerged, and he held out a small, white card to each of them. Eleanor took it.

ELEANOR BARTON: MEMBER, it said.

"Library cards?" Otto asked.

"They will allow you to return at any time, without the aid of the Wending," the Librarian said. "They are not often given out. Do not abuse the privilege."

"We won't," Otto pledged, his eyes shining at the idea of being able to get to the Library whenever he wanted.

"Humph," the Librarian said. "I am going to make tea. Editor?"

"I have something I need to discuss with Eleanor," the Editor said.

"Suit yourself," the Librarian said, and drifted out of the room.

The Editor waited until he was gone, and then she beckoned Eleanor over to a corner of the lobby. "I'm not actually authorized to do this, but here." She drew a plainly bound book from her robes. The front was labeled in neat lettering: *The Small, Cursed Town of Eden Eld, Version One (Archived).*

"We can take it with us?" Eleanor asked.

"You can use it to overwrite the version Katie has," the Editor told her. "That means you can fix things as soon as you get your hands on the other book—no need to get back here first. The draft only goes up to the eclipse, but that should be enough for the rest of the timeline to repair itself on its own."

"Does that mean the people who disappeared will be back?" Eleanor asked.

"Indeed. Everything back the way it should be," the Editor promised.

"But what about us?" Eleanor asked. "We'll still have been missing for months. Can't we go back to the eclipse?"

The Editor shook her head. "Time marched on without you, Eleanor. Broken or otherwise. Going back now would only create new problems. But I did make a minor revision for you—small enough it shouldn't cause any problems."

Eleanor opened the book to the last few pages and spotted the red-ink paragraph right away. "Everyone thinks we've been at a special boarding school in Maine?" she asked.

"You've been writing home regularly. They miss you, but they aren't worried. I made sure to put in that you've been getting excellent grades," the Editor said, sounding pleased with herself.

At least their families wouldn't be frantic. "Thank you," Eleanor said. She hugged the book against her chest. Jenny and Naomi and Lily and Pip's dad were safe within the pages of this book.

The Editor glanced over at the hedgewitch, who was looking through her bag, checking her supplies. The Editor pulled out two other books—these ones much slimmer. "And I thought you might find these useful, too," she whispered.

Eleanor looked at the titles, and her heart skipped a beat.

The Glass-Heart Girl, Version One.

Claire Barton, Version One.

"I'm afraid I don't know your father's name or origin, so I wasn't able to find his book," the Editor said.

Eleanor opened to the first page of her mother's book. *Claire Barton was born in Eden Eld to parents who tried their best to love her. Their best, alas, was not very good at all.*

"Here. To carry them," the Editor said. She handed Eleanor a tote bag with LIBRARY OF ENDERSEA 5,000TH ANNUAL POETRY SLAM printed on it. Eleanor looked over her shoulder. The hedgewitch had finished her inspection of her satchel and was turning back. Eleanor tucked the three books into the tote and slung it over her shoulder. "Thank you," she said, her voice hoarse.

"I always hope for a happy ending," the Editor said, and patted her shoulder kindly. "Good luck, Eleanor. Good luck to all of you."

Eleanor looked toward the others. They were ready, waiting for her. It was time to go. She steeled herself and reached for the Wending.

This time, it leaped into her grasp. She almost laughed in surprise—she could feel it, see it, all around her like a tapestry, every thread blazing in a thousand colors. Worlds and people, all woven together. Nothing was truly alone, she realized—everything in every world was bound to other things, other people. And she could see *all* of them.

"Eleanor, you're glowing," Otto said, sounding both alarmed and excited. Eleanor looked down at her hands. The words written on her skin were glimmering with light.

"It's okay," she said, grinning. The power shining within her wasn't frightening anymore—it was *wonderful.* It was *hers.* She stretched out her hand. "Take us home," she asked the Wending. "Please."

And the road opened. An orderly gravel path, twining right up to the front door of Ashford House.

"Nice," Pip said. She picked up the kitten-of-ashes, setting the little feline on her shoulder, and started forward. The others traipsed along behind. Eleanor followed. As she stepped between the Library and the front yard of the house, the air pressure changed, making her ears pop. It was still pitch-black, and the false night was chilly and damp.

"It's just the way we left it," Pip said, looking around.

"Not quite," Otto said. He pointed to the flower bed under the front window, which Jenny tended every spring. The daffodils had begun to come up, their blossoms still closed tight.

"It's Halloween. And the eclipse. And spring," Eleanor said slowly. "Katie didn't just keep time broken. She broke it *more.* We aren't just going to have to fight her—we're going to have to fight all three of them. Mrs. Prosper. Katie. And Mr. January."

"Aw, rats. That means I'm going to have to work," the cat-of-ashes complained.

The kitten-of-ashes laid back her ears and hissed. "Bad," she growled.

"Oh, hush. My master hasn't given me any instructions *yet.* Doubt he'll even notice I'm back for a while," the cat-of-ashes said.

"Great. This is all just great," Otto said.

"We'll prevail," Pip said. She flashed them a grin. "We're the Heroes Three for real now, right? We can't lose."

Eleanor wished she believed that.

INSIDE THE HOUSE, the color was still normal. Ashford House, it seemed, still offered some protection.

"I don't know if this will last," Otto said, peering around. "I can see the magic Bartimaeus put on the house, now. It's all patchy. And it's wearing out more and more."

"Why hasn't he fixed it?" Eleanor asked. Then she realized—the house was completely quiet. Her heart thudded in her chest. "Uncle Ben?" Eleanor called. There was no answer. "Bartimaeus? Anyone?"

Nothing.

Panic flashed through her. She ran through the Great Room, looked in the drawing room and the kitchen, dashed up each of the staircases. She threw open doors and hollered down hallways, but there was no sign of either man.

Otto and Pip were doing the same and the three of them careened into each other in the hall outside Eleanor's room, panting. The kitten-of-ashes clung to Otto's shoulder, leaving little scorch marks on his shirt.

"They're gone," Eleanor said. "They're gone and everything's gray and—"

"It's okay," Otto said. "They'll come back when we reset things, right?"

"They probably just fell through the time cracks with everyone else," Pip said in agreement, her hand on Eleanor's arm. The kitten-of-ashes chirped comfortingly and gave a raspy little purr.

Eleanor nodded, wiping tears from her cheeks. Ben would be okay. He was safe, just like Naomi and Jenny were safe, just like *everyone* was safe.

"Uh," Otto said. He was looking behind Eleanor with a pained expression. "That wasn't like that before, was it?" he asked.

Eleanor turned with a sinking feeling. Otto was staring at the grandfather clock. The clock that ran backward, that warned them when the People Who Look Away had arrived. The glass face of the clock had cracked, and the pendulum was still. The hands weren't going anywhere—forward or back. And there were too many of them.

"There are nine," Otto noted. "Three hour hands, three minute hands, three second hands."

"Halloween, the spring equinox, and the eclipse. Three times, all stacked on top of each other," Eleanor said.

"Bad," the kitten mewed once more.

Otto gave a grim nod. "I might be able to fix some of Bartimaeus's wards. I'll get the hedgewitch to help."

"I'll scout the perimeter. Make sure Katie's not already sneaking up on us," Pip said.

"What should I do?" Eleanor asked, a note of panic still in her voice.

"You got us here," Pip said, giving her arm a friendly squeeze. "Take a breath. We've got a few minutes before the world ends."

"Probably," Otto added, and Pip elbowed him in the ribs.

Otto and Pip dispersed to their tasks. Eleanor made her way down the stairs. Ben was gone. Jenny was gone. Naomi was gone, with her infectious laugh and perfect dimples. Thea was gone. For good.

She stood at the bottom of the stairs and shut her eyes. She had to stop losing people. She couldn't bear it any longer.

Cold as glass, Eleanor thought. Wander had warned her not to let her heart be broken. But then, she'd lost Wander, too—and Jack. Except . . .

Ben had said they disappeared through one of Wander's portals before time broke. That meant they hadn't been in Eden Eld. Maybe they hadn't disappeared through the cracks in time like Jenny and the others.

Maybe she could still find them. She'd pulled the hedge-witch into the Pallid Kingdom. Surely she could find her father the same way.

All those bright threads connecting things—some of them connected to *her.* And she found the two she was looking for. "Can you bring them here?" she asked the Wending. Maybe it was foolish to talk to it like it understood her, but she almost thought she felt a kindness in the Wending as she opened her eyes. A simple path unfurled before her, and she *reached,* pouring all her aching love and longing into it. The air shimmered—and Jack and Wander appeared on the road, looking bewildered. Then they spotted Eleanor.

Jack let out a cry of relief, and rushed forward to sweep Eleanor up in his arms. "Eleanor, you're alive!" he said, holding her tight.

"Jack!" she said, laughing, wrapping her arms around him to return his embrace. Behind him, the road vanished, just as Pip came charging into the room, Gloaming drawn.

"What's going on?" she demanded.

Jack released Eleanor, wheeled, and hugged Pip, too. She yelped, getting Gloaming out of the way just in time not to skewer him. Then Otto came into the room, the kitten-of-ashes on his shoulder, and there was more hugging, everyone talking at the same time.

"What on earth happened to you?" Jack asked. "We've been trying to get back to Eden Eld for months, but we haven't been able to get through."

"It might have been easier if my abilities had not abandoned me quite suddenly," Wander noted. Eleanor winced, but Wander was smiling faintly. "Your eyes are full of starlight, Eleanor. You carry the Story like it belongs with you."

Jack looked suddenly grave. "The world-walker. It has taken you, then."

"More like the other way around," Otto said. Jack looked at him, brow furrowed.

Eleanor sighed. "It's complicated. But the Stories aren't a danger to us anymore."

"How is this possible?" Jack asked wonderingly.

"They're remarkable children," the hedgewitch said. Jack stiffened, turned. He looked at her and his lips formed the name *Claire*. The hedgewitch looked at him, arms folded, expression unreadable. "Hello, Jack. Wander."

Jack's hand tightened on Eleanor's shoulder. She covered his hand with hers. "She's been helping us," she told him. He looked down at her, eyes shining with the grief she felt every time she looked at the hedgewitch. He'd loved her mother, too.

His voice was rough as he said, "I think you had better explain everything that's happened."

Twenty-Two

Eleanor sat alone in her room. She'd spent so long in this room listening to the ticking of the grandfather clock just outside that now its silence was unsettling. But even with time ground to a halt, she could feel the seconds slipping away.

The bag from the Library lay next to her on the bed, the books the Editor gave her stacked on top of it. *Eden Eld. Claire Barton. The Glass-Heart Girl.* Things lost and unwritten.

Her hand strayed toward her mother's book, but she didn't pick it up. She wasn't sure she could bear to read about all the things she'd lost when her mother faded away. Instead she picked up *The Glass-Heart Girl*, opening it gingerly.

It was like the story from *The Tales of the Gray*, and it wasn't. The princess was born with backward hands and a glass heart—a heart that contained the princess's magic. Her parents were Stories. They knew they would be taken over by the tales eventually, and wouldn't be able to protect her. They feared for her fragile glass heart, and so they taught her not to feel anything too strongly. They taught her not to love anyone, especially them.

And so when they faded, and the Stories forgot her, the princess was prepared. She felt some slight sadness, but they had kept their distance from her all her life; she felt no sorrow.

Then came the knight. She rode a silver horse and carried a silver sword and a silver bow. And she, like the princess, liked to wander. And despite herself, the princess fell in love. She loved with abandon, heedless of her parents' warning.

And then came the part Eleanor was dreading. The knight fought a dreadful beast and won—but the beast's fangs carried a lethal poison, and the knight lay dying from her fatal wound.

Eleanor knew how it ended. The knight died. The princess's heart shattered. And she learned never to love again.

But Eleanor kept reading on, and as she did, she frowned.

"Hey, Miss Studious," Pip said, knocking on the doorframe and tearing Eleanor's attention from the book. She and Otto entered, both looking as worn out as Eleanor felt. "What are you doing in here all by yourself?"

"Reading. Thinking," Eleanor said, setting the book aside reluctantly. "Waiting for a perfect solution to all of our problems to occur to me."

"Awesome. Is it working?" Pip asked. She plopped down into the chair by Eleanor's desk, elbows on her knees.

"Not so far," Eleanor admitted.

"Rats," Otto said. He plopped down onto the bed next to Eleanor, leaning back on his hands. "Maybe if we all frown at each other like we're thinking really hard, inspiration will strike."

"As long as there's no actual thinking involved. My thinker's all thinked out," Pip said. She waggled her eyebrows at Otto. "Got anything useful in your extra brain?"

He made a face. "It's not an extra brain," he said. "It's more like I've got my own search engine."

"And what does it tell you about the People Who Look Away?" Eleanor asked.

"Mostly just the stuff we already know," he said. "Plus a whole bunch of awful things they've done to other people. No secret 'how to defeat them' knowledge."

"Of course not. That would be too easy," Pip said.

"There's got to be a way to fight them," Otto said. He stood up and started pacing back and forth.

"You're the one who comes up with the plans, Elle," Pip said. "What have you got?"

Eleanor thought hard. She was the world-walker now. Pip was a skilled fighter, and Otto knew just about anything he wanted to, magical and otherwise—that had to add up to an advantage. "We can't *hurt* the People Who Look Away. But when we beat Mrs. Prosper, we didn't have to. We trapped her in the labyrinth," she said.

"Temporarily," Otto clarified. "She's probably found her way out by now."

"But temporarily is fine," Pip said. She leaned back on her hands. "Right? The deal we made with them was that if they don't get us, they don't get to try again."

Eleanor bit her lip. "What if that's not enough? They broke *time* to make us fight them all at once, right? What if they find some other loophole? A way to make it Halloween again. Or a way to get to the Pallid Kingdom that isn't *that specific door* or something."

"They'll never stop, will they?" Otto asked darkly. He sat against the windowsill, scowling.

"So we have to destroy them," Pip said. She didn't sound disappointed.

"It's the only way to stop them for good," Otto agreed. They looked at Eleanor.

Pip was right. The People Who Look Away would never stop trying to get to the Pallid Kingdom, even if they had to bend the rules to do it. The only way to save their world—to save all the worlds the Pallid Kingdom would conquer—was to stop Mr. January and Mrs. Prosper and Thea for good.

Not Thea, she reminded herself. Katie Rhodes. Thea was gone.

"Elle?" Pip prompted.

"We destroy them," Eleanor agreed, and tried, as Wander had urged her what felt like a very long time ago, not to feel anything.

"But how?" Pip asked.

Eleanor stared at the far wall. "Thea told me that her parents could Empty entire worlds. I think that's what happened to the gray world we were trapped in on Halloween. They Emptied it out except for the last scraps."

"That's terrifying," Pip said with a shudder.

"Otto, does your hedgewitch knowledge know what would happen to someone if their world was Emptied completely?" Eleanor asked.

He blinked at her. Then got his focused expression. "If you Empty a world completely, it collapses. It stops existing, and so does everything inside of it. Including people."

"What are you thinking?" Pip asked.

"We do to them what Mr. January tried to do to us," Eleanor said. "We trap them in the gray world. And then we Empty it."

"Is that—could we do that? Empty something?" Pip asked.

"Eleanor can," Otto said, meeting her eyes, his expression serious.

Eleanor nodded. "The world-walker is all about connections, but it's not just *connecting.* I can pull things out. Like when I brought the hedgewitch to us. Or when I pulled the Stories out of the books and put them into us. I've never tried to Empty a world, obviously, but I think that I could. If I tried."

"Could you, though?" Pip asked. She looked intently at Eleanor. "I'm not talking about the magic. I'm talking about *you.* This would destroy the People Who Look Away. *Kill* them. Could you really do that?"

"If it meant saving everyone? Yes," Eleanor said.

"We'd have to trap them in the gray world long enough for you to do it," Pip said.

"Okay," Eleanor said. "So let's back up. Make the plan. What's step one?"

"We could—" Otto started, but Pip held up a hand to stop him.

"Step one," she said seriously, looking at both of them, "is remembering that we are in this together. The three of us. We have beaten everything the People Who Look Away have thrown at us. We'll beat this, too."

"Because we're the Heroes Three," Eleanor said with forced levity.

"No. We're Pip. And Eleanor. And Otto," Pip said. "That's all we ever needed to be. You were right, Eleanor. We're going to win this because we're *us*."

"Because we're us," Otto agreed.

Eleanor gave a small smile, trembling but true. "Because we're us," she echoed.

"Though the magic sword doesn't hurt," Otto added. They laughed, and for a moment, it didn't matter that they had Stories coursing inside of them, that there were villains prowling outside. They were just Pip and Otto and Eleanor, and they were friends, and they were enough.

Twenty-Three

They sat and talked and planned. And when they were done, they went to find the others. Pip went to talk to Jack; they would be working together. So would Otto and the hedge-witch.

Eleanor went to find Wander.

She didn't have to go far. The strange, dreamy woman was in the drawing room, where Jenny painted when the light shone through the windows in the afternoon. She was looking at one of Jenny's unfinished paintings—a forest with a crescent moon shining between the trees.

"Wander?" Eleanor said as she entered. Wander lifted one of her hands, so odd-looking, turned the wrong way on her wrists, and touched a finger to the canvas. One of the half-painted trees filled itself in at her touch.

"You've been planning," Wander said. "That has never been my strong suit. But each of us is different. Each telling of the

Story is its own. You'll be the last. The Story will fade into you, and find its end. I'm glad."

"I wasn't sure you would be. The hedgewitch was pretty angry to lose the Story," Eleanor said, drawing closer. She had the tote bag over her shoulder, her hand wrapped around the strap.

"My name is Wander for a reason, Eleanor. I don't like to stay in one place too long. And I have been the world-walker for a very, very long time indeed. It's time for a new journey." Wander turned at last and smiled at her. "But that's not why you're here. You need my help, don't you?"

Eleanor nodded. She explained, briefly, what they had decided about Emptying the gray world. "I'll open the way to the gray world. We'll drive the People Who Look Away through—Pip and Jack can do that, and Otto is going to work out a few tricks with the hedgewitch, too. But then we have to make sure they're trapped in there. That's where you come in. I was thinking you might be able to do something with your moonlight thread. If you can still make it."

"I can. That trick belongs to me, not the Story," Wander said. "I should have enough thread left over. Is that all you need from me?"

"That should do it," Eleanor said. But she hesitated. "Wander. When we were in the Library, the Editor gave me something. Something that belongs to you."

"Oh?" Wander asked. She folded her hands lightly in front of her.

Eleanor reached into her bag and drew out the book. *The Glass-Heart Girl.*

Wander stared at it. Eleanor stepped forward. Wander took a half step back. "It's your story, Wander. The original you."

"I can see that," Wander said, her hands still clasped together.

"The Editor gave it to me—yours and my mother's. I thought you would want it," Eleanor said. "You could take it. Get your memories back. You could be yourself again."

Wander shook her head. "Eleanor, I *am* myself. Not the person I used to be, no—but everyone changes. Some change more than others. I won't undo what I've become."

"But you would know who you were. You would remember your life," Eleanor said.

"What life? I was born with backwards hands and a glass heart. I made the mistake of falling in love, and my heart shattered. Why would I want to remember that?"

"But that's not what happened," Eleanor said.

Wander's head tilted curiously. "How do you mean?"

"If you read it—" Eleanor said, holding out the book, but Wander stepped back again as if she were afraid it would bite her.

"Just tell me," she said. Eleanor had never heard Wander sound afraid, but now she did.

"A lot of it is the same," Eleanor said. "Everything you said about the beginning was true. The princess was born with hands turned backward and a delicate glass heart that contained all her magic. But you were wrong about what happened when your heart shattered."

Wander looked away. "It still hurts, Eleanor. Did you know that? Every shard of it still echoes with that pain, and no Story can erase it." Around her the glass drifted, the moonlight reflecting off of it. Eleanor had once thought the little motes looked like stars. Now she thought they looked most of all like tears.

"'*Her heart shattered,*'" Eleanor whispered. "'*And all the magic it contained spilled out. Magic is just power. It can't do anything on its own. It needs purpose. But this magic had been taught a single purpose: love. All the princess's magic flowed into the knight, and washed away the deadly poison.*' The knight lived, Wander. And they kept traveling together for years. Until the Story stole the princess away."

She held the book out, open to an illustration. A princess with long dark hair and silvery shards dancing around her, held in the arms of a woman in armor with red hair and a kind smile.

Wander reached out. One fingertip traced the line of the knight's jaw—and then her hand dropped to her side again. "It doesn't matter," she said.

"How can that not matter?" Eleanor demanded. "All the things you've said about how you shouldn't love and shouldn't feel things—they're not true. We shouldn't cut ourselves off. That's the whole point of the world-walker—to *stay* connected. Even when it hurts. Because it's worth it. It's worth it even if you shatter. Even if . . ." She trailed off, tears choking her words to silence. "Don't you want to know the name of the woman you loved?"

Wander's expression was pained. "Why? She's gone. Remembering her would only hurt."

"You're already hurting," Eleanor said. "You just told me. Every shard aches."

"Because I let myself love once. Why make the same mistake again?" Wander said.

"Loneliness hurts, too. More than anything. Before I came to Eden Eld, I was completely alone. I was shattered, but I'm not anymore. Maybe you don't need to remember all the adventures you had before you were the world-walker. But I think you should remember love."

Wander looked at Eleanor for a long moment. Then she cupped Eleanor's cheek, the faintest smile on her face. "You are a sweet girl, Eleanor."

"Why does that sound like a no?" Eleanor asked. Her heart was breaking for Wander, for the girl she'd been. But her heart *should* break, she thought fiercely. Sometimes you had to shatter before you could be whole.

"If I am to remember love, I need to find it on my own," Wander said. "Those memories don't belong to me anymore. I think, in fact, they are meant for someone else entirely."

"What do you mean?" Eleanor asked.

"It's just a feeling that I have. You have that book for a reason, but I'm not it." Wander bent and kissed her forehead. It left an imprint of cold against her skin that faded slowly. "Hold on to it. When you find who it belongs to, you'll know."

With that, Wander straightened up and drifted past Eleanor. Eleanor stood with her arms folded over the book, struggling against the urge to cry. She wasn't sure who she would be crying for—Wander, walking away from her memories, or the princess whose heart had first shattered, or even the knight, left alone when the Story consumed the woman she loved.

The hedgewitch's voice broke through her sorrow with cold, harsh words. "So, Eleanor. Planning to kill me?"

Eleanor blanched, turning. The hedgewitch stood in the doorway; Wander must have passed her on the way out. Eleanor wondered how long she'd been there. "What? I'm not going to kill you," she said.

"I saw what the Editor gave you," the hedgewitch said. "I heard you talking to Wander."

"I don't want to *kill* anyone," Eleanor protested.

The hedgewitch stalked forward. "You want to undo everything I've become. You want to remove me, and have your mother back in my place."

"I—I don't—" Eleanor wanted to say it wasn't true. But she would have been lying. Of *course* she wanted her mother back. Of *course* she wanted to undo everything that had happened to her. "I don't want to kill you," she whispered. That much was true.

"If you used that book to change me back, I would be as dead as your mother is now," the hedgewitch said. There was a curious expression on her face, and when she continued, her voice was rough. "Claire did the work of raising you, but I protected us, you know. I was the parts of her that knew how to make charms and spells to keep the January Society away from us. When you were a baby . . ." She hesitated.

"I thought you didn't remember stuff like that," Eleanor said.

The hedgewitch's brow creased. Her voice softened. "It's more like it was a story that was told to me. I know that your mother was always very, very afraid. I tried to take away the parts of her that made her afraid, but she only got more frightened. I think I made your childhood very difficult, Eleanor, and I'm sorry about that."

Eleanor looked away, blinking back tears. It must have been terrifying for her mother, fighting against the Story taking her over, knowing that if she failed, she wouldn't be able to watch over her daughter. And in the end, her worst fears had come true.

"So tell me, Eleanor. What are you going to do with that book?" the hedgewitch asked quietly, her tone impossible to read.

Eleanor hesitated. She wanted her mother back more than anything else in the world. And it would be so easy. This was the Claire Barton that was *supposed* to be. All the parts the hedgewitch had erased. She would be setting things *right.*

Eleanor met the hedgewitch's gaze. The woman who was not Claire Barton stared back at her, like she was daring her to do it.

"Otto needs your help. For the fight," Eleanor found herself saying.

"Ah. Then I'm useful a little while longer," the hedgewitch said. She was smiling, but there was no warmth in it.

"I need to go find them," Eleanor said, her heart pounding.

"I'm not stopping you," the hedgewitch said.

Eleanor ducked her head and hurried out of the room, a sour taste in the back of her throat. Should she have done it? *Could* she?

She didn't know the answer. And she didn't know what she wanted the answer to *be.* She didn't like the hedgewitch—but she wasn't evil. Her mother deserved to live—but the hedgewitch didn't deserve to die. If she wouldn't force the book on Wander, she had to give the hedgewitch the same choice, didn't she?

Eleanor didn't want to kill her. She didn't want to kill *anyone.*

But she'd have to, she realized. For their plan to work, she would have to destroy the People Who Look Away. And for all the cruelty they had visited on Eden Eld and on Eleanor and her friends, the thought filled her with bitter dread.

ELEANOR SAT ON the back steps, staring out at the silent orchard. The cat-of-ashes padded out beside her and sat, curling her tail around her paws. "You all right, kitten?" she asked.

"Not even a little bit," Eleanor confessed.

The cat-of-ashes bumped her head against the side of Eleanor's shoulder with enough force to make her wobble. "You're a tough cookie. All three of you are—and sly as cats. I wouldn't have put money on you making it past Halloween, and here you are. Whatever your plan is, I'd say the smart bet is on you pulling it off."

"You don't even know what it is," Eleanor said. They hadn't told the cat anything more than what they needed her to do. It was too risky—if Mr. January asked her directly, she'd have to tell him. But she knew her part.

"I've got a good feeling about it. Besides, if you mess up, there's always your other eight lives," the cat said.

"Humans don't have those," Eleanor reminded her.

"That's right. I keep forgetting what ridiculous creatures you are," the cat-of-ashes told her, deadpan. Eleanor wrinkled her nose in amusement. "I'd better hit the road. Look out for the pip-squeak for me, will you?"

"I'll see you later," Eleanor said.

"See you on the other side," the cat-of-ashes agreed. She paused, like she wanted to say something more, and then she flicked her tail and launched herself off the step. She bounded off into the darkness, and quickly vanished.

Eleanor wasn't alone for long. Pip and Otto emerged from the house and settled on the steps to either side of her. None of them said a word for a long time. Together they stared out at the unnatural night.

"This is it," Pip said at last. "This is really it."

"Whatever happens, this is the last time we have to face Mr. January," Eleanor said. "We break the curse . . ."

"Or it breaks us," Otto finished.

"We'll win," Pip said confidently.

"How can you be sure?" Eleanor asked.

Pip shrugged. "I just am. Maybe it's the Story, but I can just feel it. We're going to be okay."

"I wish I felt that sure. I know way too much about the things that can go wrong now," Otto said. "It turns out that endless knowledge is really bad for anxiety."

Eleanor squeezed his shoulder. "I don't know if we'll win. But I'm sure about us. I'm sure about you two, and my parents, and even Wander and the cat-of-ashes. Both the cats-of-ashes. I'm sure we're together and I'm sure that we've done everything we can. If that isn't enough, then nothing would have been."

"Hey, guys?" Otto said. "Maybe this is really cheesy, but . . . I love you."

"I love you, too, Otto," Eleanor said with feeling.

"You mean you love Andy Park," Pip said teasingly.

"Wait, I thought she liked Mabel Cox," Otto said.

"Oh, shut *up*!" Eleanor cried, and then they all burst out laughing. Eleanor put an arm around Otto, and one around Pip, and pulled them both close. "Is it weird to say I'm glad I moved to Eden Eld? Even with the curse."

"It's not weird," Pip assured her.

"You have to say it, too, Pip," Otto said.

"Say what?" Pip asked, feigning cluelessness. And then she leaned her head against Eleanor's shoulder. "I love you, too," she said softly.

Eleanor didn't need the world-walker's gifts to sense the bond between them, blazing bright in the darkness.

Then Otto stiffened. "They're coming," he said.

Eleanor didn't have to ask how he knew. She felt it, too. A prickling over her skin. A chill in the air. The People Who Look Away were close.

"It's time," Eleanor whispered.

"We're ready," Pip assured her.

Eleanor hoped she was right.

Twenty-Four

Wander, Jack, and the hedgewitch emerged from the house. Jack had a sword at his hip—not Gloaming, but one still a little bit magical in its own right. Wander had looped the silver moonlight thread around her wrists, and it gleamed in the dark. The hedgewitch had her bag over her shoulder.

"They'll be here any minute," Eleanor said.

"We will be with you," Wander promised. Jack didn't say anything—but she could see in his face everything he wished he could have said. They'd barely had the chance to get to know each other, but he had been the best father he could in that short time.

And if they won, they'd have all the time in the world to spend together.

She looked at the hedgewitch. "You can do this," the woman said firmly, fiercely. Her mother would have told her she loved her. Would have given her words of comfort. But right now, she found that the hedgewitch's stern gaze was what she really needed. Because the hedgewitch didn't say things she didn't believe. She didn't say them out of hope or optimism or to make you feel better. She believed in facts. And if she thought they could win, maybe they would.

Eleanor took a deep, steadying breath. "This is the part where we have some kind of stirring speech," she said. "But I can't think of one." She let out a shaky laugh, her nerves getting the better of her.

"We don't need a speech," Pip said.

"We already know everything that we'd say," Otto told her.

"You've already been through the Wending together," Wander added.

"And faced mud beasts," Jack said.

"And survived your thirteenth Halloween, when none of those before you could," the hedgewitch reminded her.

Eleanor swallowed. "Then there's nothing left to say. We do this. Together. Win or lose, we see it through," she said.

"We're ready," Pip said. She drew Gloaming. The blade flashed in the darkness.

"We're ready," Otto agreed, patting his backpack, which was bursting with potions and tinctures and tricks.

The hedgewitch stepped forward, slipping her bag off her shoulder. "Eleanor. You'll need this." She settled the bag over Eleanor's shoulder and smoothed the strap in place, her fingertips lingering in an almost affectionate touch. "I enchanted that bag myself. When you reach into it, you'll find whatever you need right away, and nothing inside will ever be lost or damaged. It will keep them all safe for you."

Surprised by this unexpected bit of kindness, Eleanor looked inside the bag. Instead of the hedgewitch's potions and charms, the bag held a long skein of moonlight thread—and the three books from the Library. She gave the hedgewitch a startled look. Eleanor had left the books in her room. The hedgewitch could have hidden Claire's book—or destroyed it. Why hadn't she?

The hedgewitch stepped back. Eleanor shook her head. She didn't know what to think or feel—and there wasn't time to figure it out.

She turned back around. Otto and Pip caught her hands briefly, a single second of contact. Their hands dropped away quickly, but even that fleeting touch steadied her.

In that moment, Mr. January appeared at the edge of the light.

He did not step out of the shadows; he was simply there, facing away from them. And then his sisters appeared to his left and right, maybe twenty feet apart from one another. It was like the darkness had peeled back to reveal them.

Mrs. Prosper turned. Eleanor could see traces of Melia in her features, but they had grown more precise, more perfect. She looked at them with poisonous hatred. In the trees behind her, large, shadowy shapes moved, and Eleanor thought of the massive, mushroom-infested mucks with a thrill of fear.

Katie turned, and as she did, two other versions of her stepped free. They each stretched out a hand as Rag-a-bone and

Shatterblack prowled up to flank them. One held the Editor's quill, the other her inkpot. The Katie in the center had the book of Eden Eld clasped under one arm. A small satchel hung over her other shoulder.

And then Mr. January turned neatly on his heel, with a flourish of his cane. He peered at them with a twisted smile. With a *clack-clack-clack* of bones, the rattlebird swooped in, landing in the branches above him. The graveyard dog paced out of the darkness, a growl rumbling in his broad, deep chest.

"Well. Here we are," Mr. January said, smooth as anything. "This isn't what I had planned, of course, but it's a marvelous bit of innovation on my sister's part, don't you think? She's caught us up on all the tricks you got up to in your absence."

"Did she tell you that we met you, Ash?" Eleanor asked.

To her surprise, he visibly recoiled. "That is not my name. It has not been for a very long time," he said in a low, dangerous voice. "My timeline does not include your little excursion. And soon all will be put right, as if it never happened."

"We saw what happened to you there. Why would you want to go back?" Eleanor asked. The others glanced at her. This wasn't part of the plan. But she wanted to understand.

"We were young and weak. Our parents taught us to be strong," Mrs. Prosper said.

"And they will reward our return," Mr. January added. "We will have our thrones beside theirs."

The Katies said nothing.

"Now," Mr. January said, his voice getting smooth and calm once again. "May I suggest you surrender? You see, now that you've given us the gift of breaking reality, we have all the time in the world. Even if you somehow wriggle your way free now, we'll only come after you again. And again. And again. Instead of all this struggle, you could simply . . . step through the door."

He moved slightly to the side and waved his cane behind him. The darkness seemed to ooze back a little farther. From the shadows, a door knit itself into existence. It was plain, without even a frame around it, and when it swung open, it left a straight-edged hole.

On the other side, gray mist seethed, formless and empty. Eleanor shivered. The gray world. They'd been through that door on Halloween. And now it was Halloween again—more or less.

At least this meant she wouldn't have to open the way to the gray world herself.

"So what do you say? Step right in, and this can all be over," Mr. January said.

"Not a chance," Pip replied.

Mr. January shrugged, like it didn't particularly matter to him one way or the other. "Just thought I'd offer. In that case . . ." He paused for dramatic effect—but whatever he was going to say, he didn't get the chance.

"Get 'em," Pip said simply—and Eleanor and the others charged.

For a moment, the People Who Look Away seemed so surprised they didn't move at all. The second after that, everything erupted into chaos.

The three dogs were the first to react, leaping to meet the charge. Jack surged out front to meet the graveyard dog, driving him back with a sweep of his sword, while Wander danced in with her moonlight thread, wielding it like a whip the umbral hounds skittered away from.

The cat-of-ashes plodded forward reluctantly and hissed in an almost apologetic tone as she advanced on Eleanor. A tiny gray shape zipped out the back door and darted straight toward the big cat. She halted in surprise as the kitten-of-ashes launched herself, all fangs and pinprick claws, straight at her.

"Oh, for the love of—" Eleanor heard her say, and then, "Ow! Ow! Ow! You little brat, stop that!"

The cats staggered off toward the orchard, dodging and flipping and yowling.

The rattlebird launched into the air, only for Otto to chuck a glass bottle right at it. The bottle broke against its chest, and glowing vines burst out, wrapping the rattlebird's wings up tight and sending it crashing to the ground. The hedgewitch and Otto fanned out, both of them with intent expressions of concentration.

From the orchard lurched the mushroom-covered bodies of the bearlike mucks, but Pip was ready, moving to intercept them.

The People Who Look Away hung back—as always, content to let their beasts do the hard work. Eleanor kept her attention focused on Katie. She had to get the book, quill, and ink back from her.

Eleanor started forward, jaw clenched. A muck reared up in front of her. It was huge, with wide, tattered ears like a bat. Bare ribs protruded through the mud that coated its body, mushrooms growing between them. It raised a huge paw, claws extended—and then a glass bottle shattered against its torso, brilliant white light spilling out. It let out a strangled sound and crumpled to the ground, turning to dust and mud.

The hedgewitch appeared at her side, another bottle already in hand. "You okay?" she asked, a bit breathless.

"Fine," Eleanor said curtly.

The hedgewitch nodded sharply. "Go. I'll make sure nothing touches you," she said.

Eleanor ran forward again, trying to ignore the shapes lunging out of the dark, the yelps and growls and shrieks, the clash and clang of metal. The Katies were right ahead of her, watching her approach with a kind of detached curiosity.

"What arc you doing?" the one on the left asked.

"There's no point to all of this," the one on the right said.

"You won't get away," the one in the center said.

"No one ever does," they chorused together, and their voices were suddenly full of anguish and sorrow and anger.

"You did," Eleanor said. "You escaped."

"No. I didn't. I tried a hundred times, and I never did," they said. Their outlines shook, flexing. They snapped back into a single woman, then split into three again.

"You escaped with us," Eleanor insisted, tears in her voice. "You were Thea and you got away."

"That wasn't real," the center Katie said. "Enough of this." She wrenched open the cover of the book. The three of them moved in unison—one holding the ink, the other the quill, the third the book. Eleanor lunged forward, trying to cross the last distance before Katie could—

A hand closed around her wrist. "Got you," Ms. Foster spat, as all around them familiar figures appeared out of thin air—thirteen men and women. Pip's dentist. Otto's great-aunt. They were the thirteen men and women of the January Society, who had tried to hand them over to Mr. January last Halloween.

Katie, satisfied, merged once more into a single version of herself. She tucked the ink and quill into the bag that hung over her shoulder, and the book she held under one arm, surveying her work.

"Ah! Excellent!" Mr. January cried, as the Society members looked around in confusion. "A chance to redeem yourself. Get those children through the door, and all will be forgiven! I'll even let you exist again!"

"Come on, Eleanor dear," Ms. Foster said, dragging her toward the door.

The hedgewitch stepped up behind her, uncorked a vial, and dumped it over Delilah Foster's perfectly coiffed hair.

Ms. Foster gasped and spun. "Claire? What did you—" she started, and then she stopped. She didn't just stop talking—she stopped moving. Stopped blinking. Stopped breathing.

It took Eleanor a moment to realize what had happened, since everything was already gray. Delilah Foster had turned to stone.

"I should have done that before you ever had the chance to come after us," the hedgewitch growled. Eleanor grinned at her, and she grinned back.

The moment shattered a half second later as an umbral hound slammed into the hedgewitch, taking her down to the ground. Eleanor yelped and lunged to help, but a muck lurched between them. She scrambled back—then dodged under the reaching hands of a January Society member.

The fight had been pretty even before, but now more mucks were streaming out of the trees. The January Society members weren't armed, but there were a dozen of them, and three had hold of Pip, hauling her backward toward the door as another two charged a shouting Jack, seemingly heedless of his sword.

Eleanor didn't have time to look for Otto, or for Katie and her book and ink—she ducked and dodged and ran and spun as mucks and men and hounds seemed to come from all directions. The dark was closing in.

Time, already fickle, seemed to seethe and slow around her. She blinked, watching the battle as if it was in slow motion. They were going to lose, she realized, as Jack collapsed to one knee, Mrs. Prosper twisting her hands in a spell to make the roots of the trees wrap around him.

As Wander staggered, fending off the rattlebird, who must have freed himself.

As somewhere, Otto gave a scream that might have been fear or pain.

This was going to be it. Their grand plans, their months of struggling and surviving and beating the odds. It was all going to be for nothing. The People Who Look Away were going to win, and the gates of the Pallid Kingdom would open, and all the Empty would spill out.

A growl sounded behind her. She turned slowly. Rag-a-bone crouched, ready to leap. And Eleanor stood frozen. She couldn't get away. Even if she got away from Rag-a-bone, the January Society would get her. Or Mrs. Prosper, or Mr. January, or the graveyard dog. Maybe they'd already gotten the others. She couldn't see them anymore. Not Otto or Pip or the hedgewitch or Katie.

She couldn't *see* them, she realized, but she could *feel* them. She was connected to each and every one of her friends, and there were their threads, tugging at her. They were still here. They were still *alive.* And she wasn't Empty. She wasn't alone.

She closed her eyes. *Otto,* she thought, and reached out her hand. She felt his hand close around hers, as if they stood side by side. *Pip,* she thought, and there she was, too. In the middle of all the chaos, they existed in a still, perfect moment.

We can do this, Eleanor thought.

The three of us, she heard Otto's voice say.

Together, Pip's voice chimed in.

Eleanor opened her eyes. Her hands were empty, but she could still feel them, all the same.

She could feel Katie, too. *Thea.* A slight and trembling thread.

Rag-a-bone sailed toward Eleanor, teeth bared and snapping. Eleanor *reached.* She felt a hole in the world open right behind her. She stepped backward, letting it close as soon as she was through.

Thirty feet away, Rag-a-bone leaped through empty air and landed with a startled yelp. And Eleanor stood in front of Katie Rhodes. Only one of her now—ink and quill in one hand, the book in the other. Her eyes widened as Eleanor appeared.

"Impressive," she noted. "But it's not going to be enough. You can't fight your way out of your fate."

"We'll see," Eleanor said, and she lunged. Katie lifted a hand to defend herself, but Eleanor wasn't attacking. She closed both hands around the book and kept moving. She let herself fall forward, using all of her weight to tear the book out of Katie's hands.

Katie let out a cry of startled anger. Eleanor didn't look back at her. On her knees in the churned-up mud, she pressed one palm flat against the cover of *The Small, Cursed Town of Eden Eld* and reached into her bag with the other, closing her hand around the spine of the thickest book. The original, unedited version.

The Story of Eden Eld flowed through her. The small, cursed town nestled among the pines. Founded by people who had been so afraid of the world they would do anything to protect themselves from it—including sacrificing their children to Mr. January's schemes.

The words raced over her skin as they passed through her, into the book on the ground, leaving only scraps of the Story lingering in her mind. She glimpsed the names and faces of the children who had been lost to the curse before them. Some had tried to escape. Some hadn't ever realized what was coming for them. All of them were lost.

And every time they were, the same words repeated. *The three children were lost to the curse of Eden Eld. But perhaps the next three would be the ones to end it.*

And then, finally, after twelve repetitions, twelve sets of children sacrificed: *The three children had survived the curse, for now. But more trials were to come, and only time would tell whether they could end the curse for good.*

We can, Eleanor thought, as the last of the story swept out of her and into the book. *We will.*

Katie grabbed her by the hair, hauling her up. The book fell from her hands to the ground.

For a moment, Eleanor thought it hadn't worked. It was still dark as night.

And then she realized that the moon was shining overhead. It wasn't dark *as* night. It *was* night. Halloween night. Any signs of spring withered and vanished. The apples on the trees swelled, some falling rotten to the ground. The January Society dissipated like so much fog, their fates restored as the timeline reverted.

The mucks fell back. The umbral hounds retreated with quizzical growls.

The air filled with the familiar *tick-tock-tick* of the grandfather clock—and in the house, a baby began to cry.

Eleanor twisted to smile triumphantly at Katie. Katie released her grip and fell back a step with a shocked expression, eyes roving over the rapidly changing scene.

Otto, Pip, if you can hear me, I have an idea, she thought, sending the words along the connections between them. She felt their understanding on the other side.

The world-walker Story was still flowing in Eleanor's veins, its words written on her very soul. She stretched out her senses and turned. Mr. January and Mrs. Prosper looked about in rage and confusion as they guarded the door. Pip and Otto were running across the muddy, torn-up battlefield. Elsewhere, Wander was helping Jack to his feet, and the hedgewitch leaned against a tree, panting heavily with mud splattered across her body.

Otto crashed into Mrs. Prosper, and the elegant woman toppled backward. Pip drove Mr. January backward, retreating from her slashing blade. And Eleanor reached out in that instant, nicking tiny holes in the fabric of the world for the two villains to fall through. They stumbled through one portal and out of another—straight through the door to the gray. Pip leaped through the portal after Mr. January even as he regained his balance. He lunged for the doorway—but Pip slammed the door shut right in his face.

She spun and put her back to the door, digging her feet into the ground to brace it. Wander hurried toward her, unspooling the moonlight thread.

Eleanor turned to Katie, who stared at her with a weary kind of anger. "So you did have a plan after all," Katie said, contempt in her voice. "You won't put me through that door."

"I don't have to," Eleanor said. "I can make my own."

The tiny portals zipping across the battlefield had been easy. Opening a door to the gray world was harder—but the world-walker whispered, and Eleanor listened, and the portal stitched itself together behind Katie.

"I'll take that," Eleanor said. She reached out, grabbing hold of the strap of Katie's bag, and with the other hand she shoved her hard in the chest, throwing all of her anger and sorrow and fear and triumph behind it.

Katie fell back. The strap of the bag snagged for a moment, and then came free, and she fell backward. Into the portal. Into the gray.

Now close! Eleanor thought, and the portal sealed shut. The gray—and Katie—vanished. Eleanor grabbed the moonlight thread from her bag, a needle already affixed to the end, and began stitching up the air where it had been. A moment later and Wander was beside her, her stitches elegant next to Eleanor's haphazard zigzag.

"Almost," Wander whispered. "Almost—"

Eleanor could sense the connections between the worlds cinching shut. A gap, a crack, a sliver, barely a whisper—

Just as the opening between the worlds shut, something wrenched it open. The door opened—just a bit. Just enough for Katie Rhodes to lunge out. To wrap her hand around Eleanor's throat.

To pull her through the door, into the gray, as the link between the worlds was stitched shut.

Twenty-Five

Entering the gray world was like going blind. Everything lost its definition. There were no edges, no shapes, no shadows. Just flat and endless gray.

Gray, and the People Who Look Away. Mrs. Prosper was picking herself up, dusting off her skirt. Mr. January stood leaning on his cane and glaring at Eleanor, still held in Katie's tight grip. Her breath rasped as Katie's fingers squeezed her throat, and she grabbed at the woman's wrist, trying to break her hold.

"What have you done?" Katie snarled.

"Open the door, sister. We are running out of time," Mr. January said impatiently.

"I can't. They've done something to seal us off," Katie said.

Eleanor struggled to breathe. Katie held her just off the ground, so her toes barely touched. The gray around them was slowly starting to take shape—the faintest suggestion of tree trunks rising from the formless color.

She had to get out of here—but she couldn't. She was as trapped as they were.

"Then *unseal* us," Mr. January said.

"I can't," Katie growled. She dropped Eleanor and gestured sharply. The gray seethed over Eleanor's wrists and ankles, turning solid and pinning her in place. Eleanor gasped, her lungs greedy for air, and then broke out coughing. Katie looked down at her in disgust.

"Don't just stand there. Do something," Mrs. Prosper snapped. "Time is moving again. If midnight comes, we'll have lost our last chance."

"Ticktock, little sister," Mr. January chided. "Honestly, if I didn't know better, I would suspect you didn't *want* to get home."

Katie scoffed, but Eleanor saw the brief flash in her eyes—old fear, old hatred. This Katie had never escaped the Pallid Kingdom, but she'd wanted to. They all had, once. The difference was, *this* Katie remembered what it had been like to be free. If only for a little while. A few hours of kindness.

Maybe that was enough. Maybe Thea wasn't completely gone, Eleanor thought—maybe she could still be saved.

"It's no matter," Mrs. Prosper said, rolling her neck. "If we must move on, we will. We'll find some other way."

"Says the woman who already squandered her chance. I'm still in the game," Mr. January said.

"I'm only saying it doesn't hurt to start thinking of next steps," Mrs. Prosper said.

"You made a deal," Eleanor said, drawing their attention to her. Her voice was hoarse, her neck still sore from Katie's fingers. "You promised you wouldn't try to open that door again, if we won."

"*That* door. I'm sure we can find another way in," Mr. January said with a dismissive wave of his hand.

"And in the meantime, I have always enjoyed a touch of vengeance," Mrs. Prosper said, her smile small and cruel. "We never promised not to harm your friends and family, did we? Oh dear. You really should have been more thorough when you struck that deal."

Eleanor shuddered. There were so many things they hadn't thought of. But if they'd had a month to craft the perfect bargain, she was certain the People Who Look Away still would have found a way to worm through some loophole.

She could feel the gray all around her. Everything she would have to strip out of this place. She could do it even if she was inside, she was sure of it.

She would be destroyed, too. But there was no way around it. She couldn't let the People Who Look Away hurt her family, or Pip's and Otto's families.

"None of this matters, because we haven't lost yet. I am going to find a way out of here," Mr. January said. He looked expectantly at his sisters. "If anyone cares to help."

"I will. Our sister can guard the one prisoner she managed to capture," Mrs. Prosper said, voice dripping with scorn. She stepped toward him, arms crossed.

Together, the two of them set off into the gray. Eleanor could hear them long after they disappeared—they were still arguing over whose fault this whole thing was.

The gray mist was receding as the world got more real. As it faded, a huge shape came into view, looming in the distance. The door. Not the small, simple door that led back to Eleanor's own world, but the door from the gray to the Pallid Kingdom. It was huge, towering in the distance. Chains lashed it shut—thirteen chains, each secured with a heavy lock. Thirteen locks that needed thirteen keys.

Eleanor shut her eyes. She flattened her hand as best she could against the cold ground. It was gaining texture as the gray world spun itself into something like a forest. It had been like this the first time they were here, too. The longer she stayed, the more real it would become. And the weaker she would get. It wasn't a place where humans could survive very long.

Eleanor set her jaw. She'd save them. Her parents. Her friends. Naomi. *I wish I'd gotten to see you dressed up like a pumpkin*, she thought, before reaching for the essence of the gray world. She felt it, cool and lifeless, pooling around her. All she had to do was let the gray flow out of this place, and there would be nothing left. No gray. No life.

Nothing.

"*I love you, I love you, I love you*," she whispered, and she let the words sing along every bright cord that was bound to her. To Otto and Pip and her mother and Jack and Naomi and Jenny and Ben.

"What do you think you are doing?" Katie said, looking over. She leaned down, grabbing Eleanor by the throat again and hauling her upright. The gray bands around Eleanor's wrists and ankles slid free. Her concentration broke. The sense of the gray slid away from her. "You were trying to Empty this place?"

"I have to stop you," Eleanor choked out, wrapping her hands around Katie's wrists to try to break her grip.

"You'd die, too," Katie said, leaning close.

"But everyone else would be safe."

Katie scoffed. "You think you're a hero. You think you can save everyone, but you can't."

"I'm sorry I couldn't save you," Eleanor said. "I wish you could have stayed with us."

"I wish I had never met you," Katie spat. Their faces were so close that Eleanor could see every fleck of gray in her eyes. Around them, the formless gray flowed in meaningless patterns. "I spent centuries destroying every part of me that had ever loved or hoped or dreamed of something different, and then you went and plucked her out of the past. She's still in here. Her story, and mine. So I have to remember. All that sickening optimism. How she adored you. How you *failed* her. I stopped hurting a long time ago, Eleanor, but now it hurts all over again." Her voice was ragged as torn paper, and with each sentence her fingers tightened more around Eleanor's throat.

Katie's teeth were bared, her face drained of blood. Hatred blazed in her eyes.

No, not hatred.

Pain.

Spots appeared in Eleanor's vision, blotting out Katie's misery-twisted face. Eleanor wanted to tell her she understood. She knew why Katie had turned herself cold and cruel and uncaring. *Cold and clear as glass.*

She was afraid to shatter.

Eleanor tried to speak, but she couldn't breathe, couldn't make a sound. She was getting weak as she struggled to breathe, and Katie hadn't let go. *Sometimes you have to shatter,* she wanted to tell Katie. *But even a shattered heart can heal.*

She couldn't say it. But she could show her.

Her hand fell into the bag at her side, and the book seemed to leap into it. Eleanor closed her hand around Katie's wrist. Wander had said she would know who this story was meant for when the time came. And now she did.

Wander's story flowed into Katie. Not unwriting her, but adding to her story, fitting into the gaps. The words spiraled up her arm, so fast that Eleanor only knew what they said because she'd read them already.

The princess cut herself off from the world, for fear that it would hurt her. And so when her parents vanished, when she was left alone, she did not weep. When famine came across the land and everyone suffered, she did not despair. When the rains came again and the valleys and fields rang with celebration and feasts, she did not smile. She was as cold and clear as her glass heart.

Katie stood frozen as the words sank into her. Eleanor didn't stop. She couldn't stop. Not yet. Into Katie flowed the lovers' first meeting. The slow awakening of the princess's heart.

The battle. The poison. The knight, dying. The princess, weeping.

Shattering.

Healing.

She didn't stop, not until the final words snaked around Katie's wrist and vanished.

She knew when she had first spied the knight across the river, she ought to turn away. But if she could go back to that moment, she would do it again. She would shatter again. Because such love was worth shattering for, always.

Katie's hands went slack around her throat. Katie's face was pale, her breath quick.

Once upon a time, there had been three children. They weren't evil. Not yet. But their world, and their parents, taught them to be.

Taught them to hide their true faces. To lie. To turn on each other. To stop themselves from caring, because everyone they cared about was just another weakness to exploit. They'd been shattered, every one of them. But being shattered wasn't the end.

"You don't have to be this way," Eleanor whispered raggedly. "I know you, Thea. I know who you were supposed to be, and this isn't it."

A tear glittered down Katie's cheek. "I remember you," she whispered. "But it was so long ago, Eleanor."

"It was only a few hours ago," Eleanor replied, half-pleading.

A fragile thread stretched from Eleanor to Katie. It was a strange thing, three strands wound together. Two gray and cold. But one, holding the faintest shimmer of gold.

"People are complicated. They can contain lots of stories. That's just one of them," Eleanor said. "You can choose who you want to be. You're not just Katie Rhodes. You're Thea, too. And you're the girl who shattered, and kept going."

Katie touched a hand to her chest as if to feel the beating of her own heart. "I'm still the Katie who hunted you. I have been wicked, in my life," Katie said, her expression blank and lost.

"You get to choose your story," Eleanor said insistently.

Katie fell back a step. She looked upward, tears leaving glimmering streaks down her cheeks. "I don't want this to be my story. Anger and fear and cruelty."

"Then change it," Eleanor said fiercely. "Choose something else."

"But what will you choose, Eleanor?" Katie asked, looking at her with a distant expression. "You were about to destroy this world. And all of us in it."

"It's the only way," Eleanor said.

Katie drew close. She reached out slowly, and took Eleanor's hands in her own, staring down at them. "You aren't that person, Eleanor. You aren't a destroyer of worlds. This isn't the ending you're meant for. If I get to choose my story, so do you."

Eleanor gazed up at the massive door that loomed behind them. Twelve locks hung open. Only the thirteenth remained. An idea sparked in her mind, and she sucked in a little breath. Once, she had wondered if the way to stop the People Who Look Away wasn't to beat them, but to help them. Maybe she'd been right after all.

"Eleanor?" Katie asked quietly.

Eleanor looked at her. "Can I trust you?" she asked.

Katie's lips parted. Her brow creased faintly. And Eleanor saw the moment she made her decision. "Yes," she said—and the threads between them blazed with brilliant light.

Eleanor smiled. "I think I can save everyone," she said. "But I need your help."

Twenty-Six

The gray mist seethed as Eleanor and Katie gripped each other's hands. "Ready?" Katie asked.

"Ready," Eleanor confirmed. She shut her eyes. The world-walker's power shone inside her, like looking into an infinite night sky full of stars. Katie's power was more like a ripple of silk, elegant and soft. Together, they reached for the Wending.

On their own, they couldn't have slipped out past the binding of the moonlight thread—not for a while yet, at least. But together, it was easy. They wove their way between the threads of the worlds and found what they were looking for.

Pip and Otto appeared in a shimmer of air. Otto yelped in surprise. Pip had Gloaming out of its sheath in half a second—and pointed at Katie's chest.

Eleanor turned to block the blade with her own body. "Stop! She's on our side," she said.

Pip's eyes narrowed. Otto's widened in confusion. "What are you talking about? Let's get out of here and Empty this place," Pip said.

"She's different," Otto said, peering at Katie. "Her heart is different."

"We don't have time to explain," Eleanor said. "Mr. January and Mrs. Prosper will be back any minute. I have a plan. I need you to trust me. Whatever happens, okay?"

"Of course," Pip said immediately. She lowered her sword. "She's really not evil?"

"Never again," Katie said, like it was a promise to herself. She didn't look any different, at first glance. But there was a new strength to the way she stood, and a light in her eyes that hadn't been there before.

"What are you—" Otto started, but he didn't get any further before Mr. January's voice interrupted him.

"Sister. Look at this. You've collected the full set, and just before midnight," he said. He emerged from the gray, his eyes hard and suspicious. Mrs. Prosper was behind him. Eleanor stiffened and drew back toward her friends as Katie stepped out in front.

"What exactly is going on here?" Mrs. Prosper said. "What is this trickery?"

"No trickery," Katie replied. Her voice was smooth and assured, and in it, Eleanor heard an echo of Wander. "They are here to offer themselves willingly. The final key."

Pip and Otto gave Eleanor alarmed looks, but she reached back and squeezed their hands. This was the plan. It was going to be okay.

"That's absurd. Why would they do that?" Mrs. Prosper said.

"You told us last Halloween that a willing sacrifice would make a far more powerful key than an unwilling one," Eleanor said. "So here we are. Willingly. And you're going to finally get what you want."

"Are you sure about this?" Pip muttered at her shoulder.

She wasn't—but it was too late to back out now. "We're the key. The three of us. If we're willing," she said, looking at each of them in turn. Otto nodded, though his eyes were frightened. Pip gritted her teeth and dipped her chin once. They trusted her. Eleanor could only hope they were right to.

"A willing key is the most powerful kind of all," Katie said. She stretched out a hand toward them.

Power flared, invisible strands of magic wrapping around them. Otto and Pip gasped, and so did Eleanor—her skin prickled and stung, like there was electricity dancing over it.

"This is a trick of some kind," Mrs. Prosper said, frozen in place.

"No trick," Katie replied. She reached up, and Eleanor could just barely see the gray glimmer of a thread running all the way to the massive door, wrapped in chains. She looked back at Eleanor. "Ready?"

Eleanor nodded. She gripped Otto and Pip's hands tightly. Whatever happened now, they were together.

The ferocious storm of magic building on her skin began to rush away. Katie was pulling it. Sending it dancing along the thread to the massive door. Mr. January and Mrs. Prosper turned wonderingly, eagerness and disbelief on their faces.

Mr. January had spent almost two hundred years building to this moment. Two hundred years of tricks and rituals, magic and curses, to make the three of them the perfect, final key. He meant to fling the door open. To let all the armies of the Pallid Kingdom spill out into their world, and turn it as gray and miserable as their home. And now the last key was finally sliding into the lock.

Mr. January had turned children into keys, each of them a fraction of the power he needed to open that door. But he had done his work better than he realized. Not one deal, but two linked the children to the door—two bargains, and three magical trials conquered, and their own will, and their blazing love for each other. Katie didn't need to transform them into the final key. She needed only a fraction of their power to form it, and she drew it from them painlessly.

The key appeared in the lock, and turned.

Katie didn't fling the door wide. She let it open just a crack. Just a sliver. Not enough to let the Pallid Kingdom and its armies of the Empty out.

But enough to let two wayward children back in.

The chains rattled. The door eased open.

"Now, Eleanor," Katie said, her voice strained—she was trembling with the effort of holding the door that wide, and no wider.

"Wait—no!" Mr. January cried, whirling as he realized what Eleanor meant to do.

Realized it too late. Eleanor *reached* with all the power of the world-walker, letting the Story flood through her whole being as she flung everything she had at Mr. January and Mrs. Prosper. She grabbed hold of the threads that connected them to the Pallid Kingdom.

She had drawn the hedgewitch and Jack and Wander from other worlds. She'd pulled Pip and Otto here minutes ago. This was just like that—in reverse. Not pulling but *pushing.*

"It's time for you to go home," Eleanor said. Her voice was oddly echoey. She could see stars beneath her skin, as if she were becoming more magic than girl—but she didn't feel Empty. She felt the opposite. So full of love and triumph that it made perfect sense to discover there was a whole universe inside her.

Mrs. Prosper screamed in rage—and then she vanished. Only Mr. January remained, Eleanor's power swirling around him.

"Hurry!" Katie said. "I can't hold it."

Eleanor gasped, sending one last burst of power toward Mr. January. In the instant before it hit him, he smiled. He tipped his hat. And he whispered—a whisper that seemed to come from right over her shoulder.

And then he was gone. The door slammed shut behind him.

A new lock appeared on the door. It was cold and gray and sharp looking. It looked like it would cut you if you tried to touch it. Eleanor could sense it from here—and sense what

Katie had made it out of. The cruelty the Pallid Kingdom had taught her, she had Emptied from herself. She had made it into the lock that would hold the door shut.

The gray world was silent. Mr. January and Mrs. Prosper were gone.

Only the echo of Mr. January's whisper remained, twining around Eleanor, a threat and a promise.

"Until we meet again."

In the distance, a familiar clock began to chime midnight.

Twenty-Seven

They toppled back into the orchard through a hastily opened portal, one by one. Eleanor was the last one through, and she shut it behind them with a wave of her hand, mercifully cutting off the sight of the featureless gray.

For a moment, no one said anything. They stared at each other.

"Is that it?" Otto asked.

"Did we win?" Eleanor asked.

"We won!" Pip whooped and flung herself at them—and then Otto was yelling and Eleanor was laughing and they wrapped their arms around each other, too giddy for words. Their shouts brought Jack and Wander and the hedgewitch, and then there was more celebration. Even the hedgewitch put her hands on Eleanor's shoulders and smiled at her, and for a moment it was almost—*almost*—like having her mother back.

But then the hedgewitch fell back, and as Pip crushed Eleanor in another hug, she walked off among the trees.

When their celebration finally died down, Eleanor had to wipe tears from her face. They were tears of happiness, but not *just* happiness.

For the last year, they'd lived in fear. They'd survived with the knowledge that they might never live long enough to grow up, and that everyone they loved could be destroyed if they failed. If they faltered even for a moment.

The weight of that crashing off of their shoulders was a relief—but Eleanor grieved for the time they'd lost to worrying and suffering.

She grieved for her mother—the woman she once was and the one she could have been.

For the wickedness that had poisoned the hearts of the January Society, and left Pip with a mother who didn't even love her.

For the cat-of-ashes, and the lifetimes spent bound to Mr. January's cruel service.

For Katie, spending centuries without kindness.

It was like she could see all those years, all those lives. Time was a road with many branches, and it spread out before her, wild and wonderful and horrible all at once. She could feel them. All of them. A universe inside of her.

"Eleanor," Otto said in a croak. She looked down.

Stars gleamed beneath her skin. The words of the worldwalker were sharp and silver, winding among them.

"It's beautiful," Otto said. And it was. It was the most beautiful thing Eleanor had ever seen.

The words faded. So did the stars. But she could still feel them, faintly, inside her. They wouldn't stay like this, she knew. The Story and its power would adjust and dim and fade. But it would always be part of her.

They stood haphazardly among the trees of the orchard, exhausted and bedraggled. Overhead, the moon was restored to a glowing disk, the stars glimmering in a perfectly natural nighttime sky.

"What now?" Pip asked. "Is that door going to stay shut?"

"I will make sure that it does," Katie pledged. She stood a few feet away from them, having held herself back from the celebrations.

"Aren't you evil?" Otto asked her, lifting an eyebrow.

Eleanor laughed. "It's kind of complicated."

"She has my memories," Wander said, smiling. "Doesn't she?"

"I'm sorry. I know I have no right to them," Katie said, looking stricken.

"I knew they would find the home they were meant for. She isn't who I am anymore. I am glad that she can be part of you, if you welcome her," Wander said.

Katie nodded gravely. "I do."

"And if it does not grow too confusing, being both of us," Wander added.

Katie laughed. "I am very used to being more than one person at the same time," she assured her.

Wander hesitated. "There is one thing that I would know, from the pages of my book."

"I will tell you anything you ask," Katie replied.

"The name of the woman I loved. What is it?"

Katie stepped over to her, and leaned to whisper softly in her ear. Wander's eyes shut. She let out a little sigh.

"Ah. I think . . . I think that name sounds familiar. Like a dream I once had. Thank you," she said.

"We still need to go back to the Library and return the ink and quill. And there might be other holes in the Wending we caused, right? We need to—" Eleanor started. A hand settled on her shoulder, and Jack looked down at her with a fond, weary expression.

"Eleanor. There are many tasks left to perform. But I think your part in this Story is over."

Katie walked over to where her satchel had fallen on the ground, next to the book of Eden Eld. She put the book inside with the ink and quill and settled it over her shoulder. "I'll make sure that these get back to the Library," she said.

"If you will bring me with you, my thread may help to mend any lingering tears," Wander said. "And I would like to walk the worlds a little longer, I think."

"Of course," Katie said. "Now. It's time for me to write a new tale for myself. And it's time for you three to do the same. Goodbye, Eleanor. Otto. Pip. May your paths be smooth and your tales be happy ones."

She bent and placed a kiss on Eleanor's brow. It was cold, like the night air, and left a strange but not at all unpleasant sensation. Then she straightened up and turned, a road blooming beneath her feet. She and Wander stepped onto it, and disappeared.

Eleanor let out a breath. She swayed on her feet, and her father wrapped an arm around her shoulders. "Wait," she said. "Where are the hounds? The graveyard dog? We need to—we should—"

"Relax, kid," the cat-of-ashes said, trotting out of the trees. She had a ragged feather sticking between her teeth and a smug expression on her face. The kitten-of-ashes bounded behind her, fur on end with excitement. "The hounds still belong to Katie. They took off to go find her. They're not bad dogs, really. Neither is meathead there, once you get past the breath. He was just doing what he was told." She nodded over her shoulder, and the massive form of the graveyard dog skulked into view, head hanging low.

"Sorry about trying to eat you," he mumbled.

"I take it you aren't bound to Mr. January anymore?" Otto asked.

The cat's tail lashed. "Our deal ended the minute you sent him through that door."

"What about the rattlebird?" Eleanor asked.

"Oh, *that* guy was awful," the cat-of-ashes said. She spat the feather out, a rather undignified process. "Tasted awful, too."

The graveyard dog gave a rolling, bone-quaking laugh.

"Prrow," the kitten-of-ashes said. "Meow prow mew." She looked very pleased with herself, preening.

The cat-of-ashes rolled her eyes. "You did not help. You hindered. And hid. No, you are not a fierce warrior," the cat-of-ashes admonished the kitten.

"Prrow," the kitten-of-ashes insisted, then added in a tiny mew, "Fierce!"

"Ugh. Now I'm stuck raising my own continuity error," the cat-of-ashes said. "Good thing I'm going to be an *amazing* parent. Come on, Pip-squeak. We've got places to be."

"You're going?" Eleanor said.

"We'll visit," she allowed. "But we're not *pets*. We don't *stay*."

"I stay. Also sit. Also down. Also speak," the graveyard dog said.

"Hush, you," the cat snapped, and the graveyard dog huffed and dropped to the ground, putting his blocky head between his paws in a sulk.

"I guess this is goodbye, then," Eleanor said. "Thank you. For everything."

"It's been interesting," the cat-of-ashes said, which was as close to a compliment as Eleanor could expect from a cat. The cat-of-ashes arched her spine as she rubbed up against Eleanor's leg. Eleanor scratched her ears, and the cat let out a farewell purr. "Try not to stumble into another apocalypse without us."

"I think we can manage that," Pip said, giving her a final pat.

"Merfpurr," the kitten-of-ashes concluded, bashing her head affectionately against Otto's shins. And then the two of them loped away.

"What now?" Otto asked as the road vanished behind them.

Eleanor looked around. Someone was missing—the hedgewitch. Eleanor felt a zip of alarm, but then she spotted her. She'd walked off on her own, to the far end of the orchard, near the pine forest that surrounded Eden Eld.

"Give me a minute?" Eleanor asked.

"All of a sudden, we've got all the time we need," Otto said.

"Go on," Pip said.

Eleanor walked slowly through the trees. The air was cool and crisp, the moon shining overhead. She hadn't realized how much she missed that. A normal sky overhead.

"Well," the hedgewitch said as she approached, gazing off into the woods. "You won."

"We won," Eleanor reminded her. "You were amazing in that fight. I couldn't have gotten to Katie without your help. And turning Ms. Foster to stone?"

"I remember very little about that woman, but I do remember her being *awful*," the hedgewitch said, and Eleanor laughed. The hedgewitch didn't join in. "So what are you going to do?"

Eleanor looked at her in puzzlement. "Do?"

"About me," the hedgewitch said. "You needed me for the fight. Now you don't. I'm of no use to you anymore. I'm no use to anyone. You can bring your mother back, now."

"People don't have to prove that they're useful to deserve to live," Eleanor said.

"Don't they?"

"No," Eleanor said firmly. "Thinking like that is how you get a bunch of people to agree to hand their kids over to get turned into keys. When you start caring about useful more than you care about people, bad things happen. I miss my mother. More than *anything*. But I won't destroy you to bring her back. That's not who I am. It's not what she'd want."

"But what if I let you?" the hedgewitch asked softly. She turned slowly. "Eleanor, when my power left me, it was like I was hollowed out. I *was* my abilities. Without them, I'm no one. I have no friends. No family. No ambitions or grand quests. I'm . . ."

"Empty?" Eleanor whispered.

"Not quite," the hedgewitch said, her voice hoarse. "You thought that I didn't care about you. I thought the same. But traveling with you . . . Not all of Claire vanished. And her love for you was the strongest part of her. It's still here. Faint, but here. It's the last real thing about me. You should have your mother back, Eleanor. You need her. You don't need me." The hedgewitch stretched out her hand, palm up. "Go ahead. Bring her back."

It was what Eleanor had dreamed of since her mother disappeared. Having her back. Being together again. But Eleanor didn't move. The hedgewitch wasn't always kind, wasn't always pleasant to be around—but she was a person.

"Don't think of it as destroying me, then," the hedgewitch said. "Think of it as resetting me. Roll back the clock, the way you're going to do with Eden Eld. Make me the woman I used to be, before I changed."

"Everyone changes," Eleanor said. "We're supposed to change. If I had to go back to being the girl I was last Halloween, I would lose so much. And some of it would be good to forget. But some of it, I wouldn't trade for anything." She hesitated. "You were part of my mother for a long time."

The hedgewitch nodded. "From the time she was nineteen. She held me at bay for a while, but never completely."

"Then maybe it's wrong to think of you as different people," Eleanor said. "I'm Eleanor, *and* I'm the world-walker. I made it part of me. It isn't erasing me anymore. Why couldn't it be the same for you? Why couldn't you be you, *and* my mom? Part of each other. All the ways you've changed. All the things you've done. Everything you've learned. And everything you lost. You wouldn't be erased. You'd be . . ."

"Whole," the hedgewitch said, a fragile note of hope in her voice. Eleanor's heart thumped hard in her chest. The hedgewitch took Eleanor's hand gently. "I do not want to feel this empty anymore, Eleanor. I don't want to live my life knowing that so many of the best parts of me have been erased. If you can give her back to both of us, Elle, I think you have to try."

Eleanor's throat was tight. She couldn't speak, only nod, as she drew the book of Claire Barton from her bag. She held it against her chest with one hand, and with the other, she touched two fingertips against the hedgewitch's wrist.

It wasn't like weaving the Stories into herself and Pip and Otto. The sense of her mother came to her almost reluctantly, pulled up from the pages of the book. There was none of that hunger and urgency. And there was no finding places to tuck it in, no holding it back from devouring the hedgewitch. In all of the hedgewitch's empty places, Claire Barton fit. And the hedgewitch had been formed into a perfect match for Claire.

Emotion and memory sighed through her hands, flowing more easily now. There were beautiful things in those pages, love and joy, but also sorrow, and wretched fear, and Eleanor thought for a moment of stopping those pieces from lodging themselves inside the hedgewitch. But they were part of her mother, too. The good and the bad.

The lines of inked words flowed down from where Eleanor touched. They didn't stay on the skin the way the Stories did—these words were where they belonged, now. They glowed faintly as they sank into the hedgewitch's skin, vanishing.

And then it was done.

Eleanor let her hand drop. The hedgewitch's eyes were closed, her breath quick and ragged. Eleanor wasn't breathing at all. Had it worked?

The hedgewitch's eyes opened.

And Eleanor's mother broke into a wide, tearful smile. "Elle," she said, her voice hoarse. "You found me."

ELEANOR LOVED WORDS. She loved when you could find the one perfect, correct word, and when it took a thousand wonderful words to describe something. But she would never, no matter how long she lived and how many languages she learned, be able to put into words the feeling of having her mother back.

She would never be able to explain all the emotions that rushed through her in the moment her mother wrapped her up in an embrace—or, moments later, when Jack strode up, alarmed by the sound of weeping, and knew at a glance that Claire had been restored. Or when, finally, finally, her mother and her father held her in their arms, and were together.

When Claire tucked Eleanor's hair behind her ears and looked into her eyes, it wasn't just Claire. It was the hedgewitch, too. But their stories were the same story. Eleanor's mother was her mother—all of her. Everything she'd done and everything she'd been through. All the ways she'd shattered, and all the ways she'd healed. And so was Eleanor.

So were all of them.

And as Eleanor watched Pip and Otto head home to reunite with their own families, she thought about what stories their futures would hold.

Whatever tales there were to tell, they would discover them together, she thought. She looked up at the stars, and felt the starlight within her shine.

"Happy birthday," she whispered to herself, and smiled.

Epilogue

The sun rose in a clear, crisp autumn sky. It was November—which was now officially Eleanor's favorite month. She was home. Her parents were here, together. Her friends were safe. And it was November.

Footsteps sounded on the stairs. Eleanor poured two cups of piping hot coffee and took the eggs off the stove. Jenny and Ben came into the kitchen, Naomi balanced on Jenny's hip, all of them looking puzzled to discover they had company.

"Good morning!" Eleanor greeted them, holding out the coffee. "You're going to need this."

"Eleanor?" Uncle Ben said, accepting the coffee with a deeply confused expression. "What are you doing here? Aren't you in school?"

"Long story. School closed down. Something about bedbugs, I think," Eleanor said breezily. "I'm home now! Isn't that exciting?"

"That's lovely," Jenny said with a smile. "Not the bedbugs, obviously, but we've really missed you." Naomi was thrashing in her arms. Jenny set her down, and the one-year-old stomped off across the floor on her own toddlerish mission.

"I've missed you, too," Eleanor said with feeling. It might have only been a few days from her perspective, but it felt like a lot longer. Her heart squeezed when she looked at Naomi. The little girl had grown up so much while she'd been gone. She'd missed her first steps. Her first words.

But she was here now.

"There's more I need to tell you," Eleanor said.

"How did you get back? Did Jack drive you?" Ben asked, blowing on his coffee.

"Er. Yes," Eleanor said. Technically true. "Also, my mom is here."

"Claire is here?" Jenny asked, alarmed. "Is she—"

"She's fine! She's good. She's better," Eleanor said firmly. "She's out back with Jack. I asked her to let me talk to you before you saw her in person. But I promise, everything's okay now."

Jenny pressed a hand to her chest, her eyes welling with tears. Eleanor sometimes forgot that when she'd lost her mom, Jenny had lost her sister.

"Eleanor, that's wonderful," Uncle Ben said, grinning. Eleanor was briefly grateful for the effect of the Wrong Things. They didn't seem to be questioning how this all could be happening. "Any other grand surprises?"

"Well," Eleanor said delicately. "There is *one* more thing."

Naomi had stomped to the doorway, peering out into the hall. Suddenly she grinned and clapped her hands. "Puppy!" she cried.

Heavy steps echoed in the hall. A massive, blocky head appeared, eyes glowing red. The graveyard dog looked down at the chubby one-year-old. "Woof," he enunciated clearly.

She shrieked in delight.

"We have a dog now," Eleanor said, making a ta-da gesture.

"I've always wanted a dog," Ben said faintly.

The graveyard dog lay down so Naomi could reach his ears, which had suddenly become her only purpose in life. His tail thumped on the ground.

"He's going to be a very good boy," Eleanor said firmly.

"Very good," the dog agreed.

"Did he just . . ." Jenny said.

"I've always wanted a talking dog," Ben said, and sat down, clutching his coffee.

"Everything's okay, right?" Jenny asked, looking at Eleanor with a question in her eyes.

"Yes," Eleanor said, and she broke into a wide grin. "Everything is *perfect.*"

THEY MET UP in the woods near Otto's house, where once upon a time they'd hidden out, waiting out Halloween and hoping the January Society wouldn't find them.

"I think my dad is actually remembering some stuff," Pip said. She sat with her back against a tree, her coppery hair in one long braid down her back. She still had the rangy, muscular build the warrior Story had given her, but she seemed different. The fierce light in her eyes was hers alone again, and her smile felt warmer.

Otto walked along a fallen log, arms out to balance himself. "My parents, too. I tried to sell them on the bedbug story, but then I saw Lily and started ugly-crying and my mom gave me The Look and told me that it was time to explain myself. So I did, and it went . . . fine. Like, they still remembered a few hours later, and their heads didn't explode."

"I thought I was going to get away without having to explain things. Forgot about the talking dog," Eleanor said. "They *definitely* remember now. But Jack says it shouldn't be dangerous like it was before, since it built up gradually. Jenny's got a little bit of a headache, but that's it. And now that everything's over, I'm kind of glad? I didn't want them to be worried, but I'm glad I can talk about it, you know?"

"Yeah," Pip agreed, nodding.

"Definitely," Otto said with relief. "I used to tell my parents everything. I miss it."

"So things can go back to normal now," Eleanor said.

"Yeah," Pip said. She didn't quite meet Eleanor's eyes.

"Back to normal," Otto said, shoving his hands in his pockets.

Eleanor bit her lip. Slowly, she reached down and rolled up her sleeve.

Along the inside of her arm, from her elbow to her wrist, was a line of words, written in ink that gleamed as if still wet.

> *But there were many worlds yet to wander, many paths to be walked. They called to her, and eventually, she would answer.*

Pip pushed to her feet. She shrugged out of her jacket and held out her arm, and Eleanor read the words written there.

> *But a blade does not make a hero. She would have more adventures, she knew, and face dangers not yet imagined.*

Otto stepped off the log and pushed his sleeve up above his elbow.

> *Yet his curiosity was as strong as ever. The universe held too many secrets and too much knowledge for him to be satisfied living a quiet life. He would seek out new magic and new trouble soon enough.*

As they stared, the words faded, sinking into their skin, until only one remained.

Adventure.

Seek.

Wander.

And Eleanor smiled.

Acknowledgments

Writing every book is hard and wondrous in its own way, but the final book in a series has its own special magic and mischief, and *Glassheart* was no exception. The book and I were each broken in several different ways before we found our way out of the Wending together and the grandfather clock struck midnight for the final time, but in the end I hope that I have given Eleanor, Pip, Otto, Jack, Claire, the cat-of-ashes, and all the rest a proper farewell, and that I have given you, my wonderful readers, a satisfying and thrilling conclusion to this tale of curses and friendship and sinister siblings.

As I've shared before, the idea for *Thirteens* sprang from a one-shot RPG run by my dear friend Patrick Maughan, and so I must of course thank him first. Along the way, many people have helped shepherd that seed of an idea into three books and an entire heroic journey. Lisa Rodgers was the first to read and champion *Thirteens*, providing invaluable insight on that first (very) lumpy draft. Maggie Rosenthal, as she has so many times, lent her editorial expertise, transforming every draft along the way. The No Name Writing Group read drafts, untangled plot threads, and made soothing noises when I panicked—an eternal thank-you for feedback and friendship to Shanna Germain, Erin M. Evans, Susan Morris, Rhiannon Held, Corry L. Lee, Monte Cook, and Rashida Smith. And huge thanks to Lauren Spieller, agent extraordinaire, for jumping right in mid-series to help bring the story of Eden Eld to its conclusion.

As always, I am eternally grateful to the team at Viking for taking my words and turning them into a *book*. I would be adrift without the efforts of my copyeditors and proofreaders to wrangle my continuity errors and creative punctuation, so thank you to Abigail Powers, Sola Akinlana, Marinda Valenti, Alison Dotson, and Vivian Kirklin. I have been blessed with yet another fantastic cover, illustrated by Sara Kipin and designed by Maria Fazio and Kristin Boyle. Thank you also to Kate Renner for beautiful interior design. And to those who work to get the book into the hands of its readers, especially Kaitlin Kneafsey.

I am overwhelmed with gratitude to my family, who have always been my strongest supporters and biggest cheerleaders. Especially Mike: my spouse, my best friend, and my companion in all my travels. I couldn't ask for a better partner.

Finally, the biggest thank-you goes to my readers. For those who have read along with Eleanor, Pip, and Otto from that first fateful Halloween, thank you so much—these books wouldn't exist without you. Though our dear trio have earned their retirement, there are many more heroes to be found, more roads to follow, and more adventures to be had, and I hope that you will come along for the journey.